– THE HORSE –
FROM NOWHERE

Jenny Hughes

D1627733

KENILWORTH PRESS

For Robin Hughes

Also by Jenny Hughes:
The Dark Horse
A Horse by Any Other Name
The Painted Horse

Published by Kenilworth Press Ltd
Addington, Buckingham MK18 2JR

© Jenny Hughes 2000

Reprinted 2004

British Library Cataloguing in Publication Data
A catalogue record for this book is available from the British Library

ISBN 1-872119-22-0

Printed and bound in Singapore by
Stamford Press

CHAPTER ONE

IT WAS ONE O'CLOCK in the morning when the phone rang. We were fast asleep of course but I came sharply awake at the click of the receiver being lifted. Natalie slept on, arms and legs flung across her bed under the crumpled mound of duvet. I couldn't hear what her mother was saying, but the note of exasperated urgency in her voice carried loud and clear across the landing.

"Nat!" I said, fairly softly. "Wake up. I think we've got trouble."

She grunted and flung the bedcovers around a bit more but her eyes didn't open.

"Natalie." I sat on the edge of my bed and shook her shoulder.

"Gerroff!" This time she submerged completely, just one toe poking out.

I sighed and leaned towards her.

"Come on you two!" Sandra Clements snapped the light on, pulling a sweatshirt over her head with the other hand. "That was the police. Someone's called to say we've got a horse loose. He's running around in the back lane."

"S'truth!" I leapt up and grabbed my jeans. "We'll have to get him back before he heads for the road."

"That's the girl, Kate," Sandra said approvingly.

"Now wake Sleeping Beauty up too and meet me in the car."

I struggled into the jeans and bashed Natalie with my pillow. There was no time left for subtlety.

"NAT!" I bellowed. "Wake up. Your mum wants us. Now!"

She crawled out of bed, mumbling and blinking. "Whassamatter?"

I threw her old jods and a sweater and started hunting around for my socks. "There's a horse out. We've got to help catch it."

"Which horse? There can't be. All our fields are well fenced."

"Maybe it jumped out." I abandoned the sock search – why do you always find just the one? – and dragged her towards the door. "Come ON. Wellies are by the back door. I can hear the Land Rover starting up."

"They never jump out," she was still protesting but she followed me downstairs and we pushed cold bare feet into cold rubber boots and ran out to join Sandra. She let out the clutch immediately and we hurtled down the drive and into the lane.

"Who phoned the police, Mum?" Natalie rubbed the windscreen clear and peered out.

"One of the neighbours." Sandra had the headlights on full beam and was driving carefully along, scanning the grass verge. "They heard a noise, thought it was burglars and looked out to find a horse grazing on their front lawn."

"That's good," I said. "As long as they had the sense to shut their gate we've got him."

"No such luck. The idiots took one look at the hoofprints on their precious lawn and went out and shooed the poor beast away."

"So how do they know it's one of our horses?" Natalie was still grumpy.

"They don't. They just assumed so and complained to the police. I can't imagine how any of ours could get out but it hardly matters does it? Whichever or whosoever's horse it is we have to catch him before he hurts himself."

"That's right." I was hanging out of the window, screwing my eyes up to peer at every black shadow. "There! Sandra, look."

We'd been crawling along so she was able to stop gently. "Ssh. Well spotted Kate. There he is all right. Now, gently does it. Don't make a sound. We don't want to frighten him off. The main road's too close for my liking."

We slid quietly out of the Land Rover and spread out to move towards the horse. He was standing against the hedge, his head turned towards the riding school as if he could sense the other horses. There was little light, just the moon showing raggedly through a heavy covering of cloud, but the horse gleamed palely against the ink black trees. As I got closer I could see his flanks heaving slightly and knew a wrong movement could send him into another panic ridden gallop.

"Steady then. There's a good lad." Sandra's voice had taken on the gentle, calming tone she uses on frightened animals. "Poor old boy, did they chase you off then? Keep in line with Nat and me, Kate and I'll see if I can grab him. He may spin away towards you."

"That's OK." I kept my voice steady. I love horses but I'm not as used to handling them as my friend and her mother and I didn't want to do anything wrong.

The other two closed in on the horse, still talking softly to him and it looked as if he would let them lead him to safety. Just at the last minute Natalie trod on a stick, cracking it sharply in half and the runaway threw up his head and whirled away from them. I was near enough to see the panic in his eyes and near enough too, to notice the short length of rope that dangled from his headcollar. He came straight at me, moving fast, and as he sidestepped I reached out and caught the rope. The horse whickered in fear and tried to pull away but I made my voice like Sandra's and soothed him till he stopped tugging back and dropped his soft nose tiredly into my hand.

"Oh, well DONE Kate." Sandra appeared smoothly at my side and added her grip to mine. "Good boy. Poor, frightened boy." As she crooned to the horse she gave him a swift, professional once over. "Couple of minor cuts and scratches but he's all right. It was lucky Kate got you before the traffic did, young man, whoever you are."

"He's lovely." Natalie stroked his neck admiringly. "I'm sure I've never seen him around here. Where on earth has he come from?"

"I'm certainly not trying to find out now." Her mother clipped a new lead rope on the head collar. "Let's get him safe and settled for the night and we'll phone the police tomorrow. Will you walk him home for me, Kate?"

"Sure." I was pleased she was pleased with me. Sandra's not given to fulsome praise so a well done from her means you've earned it.

The horse went with me very obligingly, walking out nicely at my shoulder. I talked softly to him all the way back along the lane and he seemed to like it. By the time we turned into Falconhurst's drive and saw the light in the stable block I was already feeling quite fond of him. Sandra and Natalie had put a lovely deep straw bed down in the "sick bay" stable and fetched clean water and a nice fat haynet. I held the runaway's head while they checked him more thoroughly, then took off his head collar and left him to settle down. I slid the bottom bolt and handed the webbing halter to Sandra.

"It only just fitted, too tight really," I told her.

"And it's a filthy old thing."

She looked at it with distaste. "Nasty. He hasn't been wearing it long, that's one thing, it hasn't marked his face at all. And he's been well looked after too, so don't go worrying about cruel owners the way you do."

"I don't," I said indignantly. Anyone would think I was a softie. "I was just saying, that's all."

"And we all know what happens when you just start saying." Natalie thumped me affectionately on the back. "You nearly went for a man's throat at the County Show last year."

"He was beating his horse after a class, just for refusing a fence. And I didn't go for him – I just said ..."

"You said he was a barbaric baboon and the only reason his horse refused was that he had hands like dead mutton and a brain to match." Sandra laughed at my outraged face. "You do tend to get a little passionate, Kate, so for all our sakes don't start imagining horror stories about tonight's horse – he's fine, I promise."

I knew she was right but I couldn't stop thinking about him. I lay in bed seeing again the fear in his eyes as we approached and the grateful way he'd touched my hand when he realised I wouldn't hurt him. Natalie had fallen asleep again immediately, sprawled in her usual untidy heap across the bed. I listened to her rhythmic breathing and tried to sleep too but the worried dark eyes of the runaway horse kept coming back into my mind. After twenty minutes I gave up trying and slipped out of my bed and back into my jeans. This time I found both socks, added an extra jumper and crept quietly out of the house.

Falconhurst overlooks its own stable yard. You can look out of the kitchen window and see the horses' heads as they watch the world over their doors. I only had to walk a few yards and I was back at the big box where we'd put the stray horse.

He heard me at his door and rolled his eyes for a moment but as soon as I spoke he seemed to relax again. I stepped inside the warm, sweet smelling stable and petted and stroked him for a while.

"I'm a bit worried about that broken lead rope and that tatty old head collar of yours," I told him. "I think someone might have been trying to steal you and you snapped the rope getting away from them. If they're still out there looking for you I want to know you're safe now. And the only way to know is to see for myself."

He whickered softly as if in agreement and blew gently at my hair. I laughed and hugged him. "So if it's all right with you I'm going to stay the night. I've never slept in a stable before. If I choose a corner just promise you won't tread on me – or do anything else on me come to that!"

I'd brought an old blanket, though it wasn't really cold and I soon found snuggling down in the straw was quite comfortable. The cloud cover had cleared and the yard was bathed in thin, mysterious moonglow. It filtered into the box and picked out the clean and lovely lines of my new friend. He was, as Natalie had said, a beautiful horse, well proportioned and strongly made with a fine head and those dark, intelligent eyes. I watched him pulling contentedly at his hay, really settling to it now he had me for company. I imagined riding him, galloping across the downs, soaring over streams and hedges and – I shook myself. Dreaming was all very well but this horse was going to be claimed by his owner tomorrow and I would never, ever even sit on his back. All I could do was stay with him and make sure he was still safe and well when they came to collect him.

But as I slipped at last into a dark well of slumber, the picture I took into my dreams was of me and the runaway horse finishing a brilliant clear round and cantering joyously out of the show ring to the sound of rapturous applause.

CHAPTER TWO

IT WASN'T ANY KIND OF APPLAUSE that woke me. It was the clanging of buckets, and the cheerful whistling of Monkey as the yard swung into its early morning routine. The stray horse heard it too and looked out, dark eyes hopeful.

"Hello my lovely. Where did you come from?" Monkey's voice was kind as always and I was glad to see the bay horse didn't flinch away. "Oh, morning Sandra. Who's this then?"

"Mystery guest." I heard her laugh and start explaining about the phone call. "So we had rather a disturbed night of it. I've left the girls to sleep on, I don't suppose we'll see them for a while ..."

"Good morning." I smiled at her and Monkey over the door and pulled a few wisps of straw from my hair. "Could I give Runaway his breakfast do you think?"

"Kate!" Sandra gawped at me, and Monkey burst out laughing, his face crinkling into the deep lines that had given him his nickname. "What are you doing in there?"

"Sleeping," I said truthfully. "I had a horrible feeling someone might come after him last night so I stayed in here and kept guard."

"Very commendable," Monkey said gravely. "What were you going to do if a horse thief did turn up? Hit him with your handbag?"

"I don't have a handbag," I pointed out with dignity. "I'd have simply raised the alarm."

Sandra threw her hands up. "But why? Why stay here all night because of this horse? He isn't even ours, why should you think someone would try to steal him?"

I explained my theory about the snapped lead rope but she didn't look convinced. "Come and get his breakfast then." She ruffled my hair, dislodging more straw. "And for goodness sake don't tell your mother you spent the night in one of my stables. She won't let you stay with Natalie again."

I trotted off to mix a feed and carried it straight back to Runaway. He was delighted to see the bucket coming but stood back politely while I tipped it into the manger and he gave me a brief nudge of thanks before diving in.

"He's really sweet." I leaned on the door and looked in at him.

"He's really quality too." Sandra, as usual, was helping with all the chores. "Someone, somewhere will be going mad this morning, wondering where he's gone."

I thought how dreadful that must be and tried to feel sorry for the owner but I could only feel envious. We carried on with the mucking out and clearing up and were actually starting to tack up the ponies for the first lesson when Natalie finally rolled into the yard.

"Sorry everyone," she yawned hugely, "I overslept. Did you call me, Mum? I didn't hear if you did."

"No." Her mother handed her a bridle "Do Poppy for me, please. We had such an active night I decided to give you both a lie in. But Kate had other ideas. She was here before me. Several hours before me in fact."

Natalie pushed her fringe out of her eyes and peered at me. "Several? How come?"

"She was watchdog for our guest." Monkey pulled my hair as he went past. "Who needs a Rottweiler when you've got Kate?"

They were taking the mickey because I'm not very big. I was considered quite tall at eleven but now I'm fifteen I don't seem to have grown much. I've known Natalie since I was ten and till last year I was always half a head taller, but now she's shot up and I've stayed still. I don't mind particularly, it means I can ride the nippy little ponies at Falconhurst as well as the horses, but it does mean I get teased a fair bit.

"Why ever did you sleep in the stable?" My friend looked at me as if I was batty. I started to explain my worry but then the pupils for the first class started to arrive so we were all too busy.

About halfway through the morning Sandra

called us over to the office and asked if we'd like to call at the police station with her.

"I've got to go into town anyway," she said. "I'm taking one of our ads along to the new saddlers for their notice board. You two wanted a look at the shop didn't you?"

"Mm, please." I rubbed my hand vaguely over my face. "I haven't had a proper wash yet, mind. Does it matter?"

She looked at me and laughed. "You've still got straw in that great mop of hair. I don't mind if you don't, but ... "

"Don't tell your mother!" Natalie and I chanted in unison.

It's one of Sandra's sayings when I'm about. My own mum is lovely, but just a wee bit old fashioned about trivialities like showering and brushing your teeth and sleeping in a bed not a loose box, so we tend to gloss over some of the things we get up to at Falconhurst. My mum also thinks all horses are some kind of dangerous monster. This, luckily, means she doesn't often come to the riding school herself, and when she does, she doesn't stay long! I get enough teasing, as I've said, without mum letting me in for more by fussing about me falling off or getting dirty.

So, slightly unwashed, and with straw bits still emerging from my thick brown hair, I jumped cheerfully into the Land Rover and off we went.

14

Natalie didn't look much better, but at least she'd brushed her own hair and it's that blonde, silky sort that always looks good.

Sandra drove in her usual careful way along the lane, then braked sharply as a middle-aged lady suddenly bounced out of a gateway at the far end.

"Good morning, Mrs – er – Gray." She stuck her head out of the driver's window and smiled pleasantly at the woman.

"I dare say it is for some." Mrs Gray tightened her thin lips. "My poor husband's been out here since nine trying to repair the damage your horse did last night."

Behind her we could see the neat gravel drive and smooth lawns of her garden. A man, presumably her poor husband, was jumping solemnly up and down, peering intently at his feet as he did so. I had a mad desire to giggle. It looked as though he was trying out the latest disco craze without music.

"Er," Sandra was lost for words and I could see her lips tremble as she, too, tried not to laugh. "I don't know what your husband's actually doing, but I can assure you whatever it is, it's nothing to do with my horses."

"Don't try to be clever," Mrs Gray snapped. "He's smoothing out the hoofprints your animal's made. Everywhere, they are."

Natalie stuck her head out too and peered with interest at the leaping Mr Gray. "Is one of the prints without a shoe? The horse has lost one, and I wonder if it's in your garden somewhere?"

I thought the woman was going to explode, and Sandra shoved her daughter's head back inside the car and said swiftly, "I'm sorry if the horse has caused any damage, Mrs Gray, but what I'm trying to tell you is it's not MY horse."

"Rubbish." Mrs Gray literally glowered. "Who else round here has horses? It must be yours. We told the police so."

"I know. They phoned me and we came out and collected him. But he's not from Falconhurst."

"Then why would you collect him?" She was a very unpleasant woman and I couldn't stand her.

"To save him from being injured or even killed on the main road." I stood up and glared at her from the other window. "You should never have chased him out of your garden like that ..."

"That's enough, Kate." Sandra yanked me back in. "I try hard not to quarrel with my neighbours – the last thing I need is you with the light of battle in your eyes." She started up the engine again and said politely, "There's really nothing more to be said, Mrs Gray, except to reassure you that my horses will never cause any such damage to your property. I'm off to the police station now. Would you like them to confirm what I've told you?"

"Oh I dare say you'll charm your way out of it as usual." Mrs Gray turned her back rudely and stomped back up her drive. We could clearly hear her muttering about "dirty, smelly animals in our beautiful garden" and Sandra gripped the steering wheel so tightly her knuckles went white.

"Odious woman," she muttered, and drove off looking pink and ruffled.

"Why don't you have a real go at her?" Natalie stared at her in surprise. "Or you could have unleashed Tiger Kate here. The Grays are completely in the wrong."

"I don't want any trouble." Her mother sighed and tried visibly to relax. "If there are too many complaints from local people my riding school licence could be revoked. And we can't afford to move."

"I don't see why we should have to." Natalie thumped the dashboard crossly. "Falconhurst was here first. The Gray's grotty little bungalow was only built a year or so ago. If they don't like horses why did they choose to live near them?"

"I don't know. I suppose this area has become the suburbs, the town's crept so close in the last few years. People like the Grays move out here and pretend they're in the country, but they haven't a clue about country ways." Sandra groaned and tried to flex her rigid fingers. "And much as I'd like things to be the way they were, times change and we've just got to try not to upset the neighbours any more than we can help."

"Sorry Sandra." I felt ashamed of my outburst."I didn't mean to cause trouble."

"It's all right Kate."She gave me a brief, worried smile. "You were quite right, the Grays did behave badly but unfortunately these particular neighbours are the kind of people you can't reason with."

"Report the way they chased the runaway horse out of their garden to the police station then." Natalie very rarely gets in a rage but she was working up to one now. "Maybe the horse's owners could sue them or something. If Kate hadn't managed to grab him when she did they wouldn't HAVE a horse by now."

The horse's owners. I wondered again who they were and what they were like. They'd be so pleased to know their beautiful boy was OK. We all trooped in to the police enquiry desk and Sandra gave her name.

The sergeant looked at his notes. "Ah yes, Mrs Clements. You phoned in early this morning in response to our one a.m. call to you."

"That's right." Sandra explained how the Grays had reported a horse in their garden and told the police it must have come from Falconhurst.

"But you told my officer this morning that in fact the horse isn't one of yours." The sergeant picked up the book and read "Light bay gelding, fifteen point three haitch haitch".

"That's hands high," I put in helpfully.

"Thank you miss, 15.3 hands high, aged about seven. White snip on nose. Tee Bee Ex."

"Thoroughbred Cross," Natalie and I said together. The sergeant looked nice but you could tell he wasn't horsey.

He smiled and repeated patiently "Thoroughbred Cross. Thank you again. Well, Mrs Clements, there's nothing I can add to what we told you this morning. We're obviously waiting for someone, somewhere to report a missing horse so we can tell them we, or at least you, have found it. Till such time we can only ask you to hang on to the animal, not having the facilities to do so ourselves."

"I see," Sandra frowned. "It seems very odd no one has noticed a horse like that has gone missing."

"Just broke out of his paddock most likely. There's a few fields still around where people keep their ponies. If the owners haven't been along to look at them yet today they wouldn't realise he's escaped."

I hated to think there were people who didn't check on their horses first thing but I knew he could be right. I decided to air my theory anyway."I was a bit worried," I told him "because he had a broken length of rope hanging from his head collar. I thought perhaps someone had tried to steal him and he'd broken the rope getting away."

The sergeant raised his eyebrows. "You think he could be stolen? Again, no one's reported such a thing, and last night's phone call from Mrs Gray states the horse 'trod on rope hanging from its bridle as it jerked its head to run away'. The lady said she's got the rope to show us."

"Hoping to match it up against my lead ropes I dare say," Sandra muttered crossly. "Oh well, that's your idea gone, Kate. You've got my phone number when the bay horse's owner does eventually contact you haven't you, Sergeant?"

He nodded and bade us all good morning.

We drove on to the new tack shop and feed supplier. I was quiet because I was thinking.

"If Runaway's just wandered out of a field somewhere in the night," I said, "why would he be wearing a rope at all? Nobody turns their horse out with a lead rope on."

"Oh leave it Kate." Natalie was still in a mood because her mother wouldn't take on the Grays. "We'll find out sooner or later won't we."

"I just hope it's sooner." Sandra pulled up outside the shop and yanked the handbrake on. "I can't have this horse, nice as he is, eating his head off at my expense for too long."

It wasn't turning out to be a very happy morning, I thought, and dragged myself somewhat dismally out of theLand Rover and into the new saddlers.

Sandra and Natalie went over to talk to the owners and I browsed through the tack department, running my hand over the silky new saddles and breathing in that lovely leather smell. The shop was tiny so they'd built the shelves very high to display the bridles and stuff. It was like walking through a narrow tunnel, totally surrounded by interesting horsey things and I was completely hidden from the main counter area.

I was just admiring a smart studded browband, imagining the runaway horse wearing it as we galloped into the sunset, when someone swiftly turning the corner cannoned literally straight into me, knocking the breath right out of my body. I flopped down on a stool gasping and a worried voice said

"I'm really sorry. I didn't see you. Are you OK?"

I looked up, straight into the darkest, most fabulous eyes I'd ever seen. The breath that was gradually returning whooshed immediately away, and my heart hammered, my fingers trembled and my knees knocked.

"Are you OK?" He repeated and even his voice was great.

I wished and wished I'd washed my hair as I nodded, still unable to speak.

He put out a strong hand and lifted me up. "That's good. I'm Jason. Hello."

CHAPTER THREE

I FINALLY MANAGED to croak hello in return and tell him my name was Kate.

"And you work with horses?"

I hoped it was the professional way I looked and not the straw in my hair that told him.

I nodded. "Sort of."

"Lucky you. I don't know enough about them. I was hoping to ask the owner of this shop for a holiday job but he's talking to someone. I decided to belt down here out of the way till they've gone. And I mowed you down in the process."

"Don't worry." My breathing had returned though my heart was still thumping like a bass drum. "No harm done."

"You're sure? You're still a bit pale." His deep brown eyes were concerned.

"I'm ... " I broke off as Natalie's footsteps tapped irritably towards us.

"Kate? Where are you? Come on, we've got to go."

I turned and said, "I'm here. I thought we were going to look at the boots they've got."

"No time, apparently." She appeared round the next corner, where she could see me, though Jason was out of sight behind the bridles. "Mum's mad at me and wants to get straight back. What's the matter with you anyway? You're as white as a sheet."

I felt my face go hot and said quickly, "Someone bumped into me, that's all. I was just winded."

"Oh," she scuffed her boot sulkily along the floor. "Another moron I suppose. I bet they didn't even say sorry. I'm sick of people today."

I glanced quickly at Jason and saw his face darken. I put a hand out to him. "She didn't mean that," I began, but Natalie was already walking away, moaning as she went. "Give me horses any day. People only cause trouble. Especially people who know nothing about horses. People like that make me sick ..."

I groaned as she disappeared from sight and turned back desperately to Jason. "She didn't mean you ... " but I was talking to empty space. Jason, with his dark good looks and fabulous brown eyes, had vanished into thin air.

I wanted to find him and apologise but felt too shy to go running round the shop looking for him.

"Anyway I don't suppose he'll give me another thought," I brooded sadly and drifted back outside. Sandra and Natalie were arguing, not something they do as a rule, but they'd been building up to it all morning.

"Making you pay to put a poster up!" Natalie was glaring, hands on hips, at her mother. "You'll bring him loads of business, encouraging people to take up riding and kit themselves out. And he even made you pay to display that postcard you wrote about the stray horse."

"Which postcard?" I still felt distinctly wobbly and they both looked at me in surprise.

"You all right, Kate?" Sandra put a cool hand on my forehead.

"I'm fine," I said "What did your postcard say about Runaway?"

"Just his description and our address and phone number," Sandra said. "In case his owner doesn't think to contact the police."

"I'm sure he will." Natalie was still in fighting mood. "Everyone else phones the police. Neighbours get them to hoick us out of our beds when it's not even our horse and ..."

"Oh give it a rest, Nat," Sandra said wearily. "Why are you taking all this out on me?"

"Because you're too soft. You're letting the Grays walk all over you, you're being an unpaid horse warden for the police, you're even letting the new saddler charge you too much."

"You have to pay to advertise," her mother defended herself. "The poor man had to close a big premises and open this tiny little shop to keep costs down. He needs all the revenue he can get."

"We've all got problems," Natalie said grandly and I leaned my face against the cool glass of the car window and wished they'd stop.

I kept hoping Jason would appear. There was a bike outside which must have been his, but though it was a few minutes before Sandra stopped arguing and started driving he still didn't come out.

I thought about him all the way back to Falconhurst. Natalie and I were due to do some schooling before lunch while Sandra and Monkey took an improvers' class for a gentle hack. Monkey had been giving a stable management lesson while we were out and as usual the yard looked beautifully clean and tidy. Natalie and I tacked up her mare, Rio, and the roan pony, Amber, for our session in the school. We were both quiet, me because I had a lot to think about, what with the stray horse and whether I'd ever be likely to see Jason again, and Nat because she hadn't yet simmered down. I knew once she started riding she'd be OK. She doesn't often get mad and if she does, riding Rio soon cures it. Sandra always teaches you never ever to get angry at a horse and if you're riding it properly you should be concentrating so hard there's no room to be temperamental.

Rio, Natalie's horse, is a lovely mare, kind to handle and very beautiful, but one look at her flaming chestnut colour and excitable action and you know you've got your work cut out. Nat could take her pick of horses to ride. All the others at Falconhurst are properly schooled and well mannered, but it's Rio she loves. I've ridden the mare a few times. Well, three to be precise. She ran off with me the first time, dumped me in a ditch the second and rolled on me (luckily in the soft sand school!) the third. I now stick to Amber or Carmen and watch Natalie and her chestnut loony with fascinated horror. We were only flat schooling that day so there should have been less fireworks but as usual Rio did her drama queen act.

We'd warmed them up and were doing lateral work, starting with leg yielding and shoulder in. The horses had been going very nicely in trot, so I asked for collected canter and took Amber down the centre line to try a half pass to the right. She's a little stiff on that side and I didn't think the bend we were getting was quite uniform so I asked Natalie to talk us through it a second time. She brought Rio to halt and watched us pass from the long side to the centre line, frowning in concentration.

"Her shoulders are slightly in advance, that's good, but there should be more active forward movement," she called. "Bring your ..."

I never did find out what because, of all things, a pigeon, fluttering clumsily in that jumbo jet style they have sometimes, flew across the school, his light grey wings virtually brushing Rio's nose.

You'd have thought it was a pterodactyl at the very least from the silly mare's reaction. She threw herself sideways and upwards at the same time, an ungainly movement that jerked poor Natalie out of the saddle and down the side of the horse's neck. How she stayed on at all I'll never know but she hung on grimly, backside in the air, one hand gripping the chestnut mane and the other desperately groping for her lost reins.

Rio thundered madly round the school and eventually by a gymnastic backward wiggle and some weird bottom shuffling Nat managed to get back in the saddle and into control. She calmed the chestnut back to walk and finally to a slightly shuddering halt.

"Phew!" Her hat was over one eye and the front of her jumper twisted nearly to the back. "All that for a bird! Have you never seen a pigeon before, you peanut brain of a horse?"

I heard a slight chuckle and whipped round quickly to see we were being watched. The fenced in school is behind the stable yard so it can't be seen from the road, but there, sitting on his bike which was leaning against the back of the stable wall, was a highly amused looking Jason! I felt my face go all hot again and wondered instantly what sort of scarecrow I looked this time, with my wild hair shoved unbeautifully into a skull cap.

"Er – hullo," I said and walked Amber sedately

over.

"Hello Kate." He smiled at me and I felt my knees knock again.

Lucky I wasn't riding Rio – she'd have taken that as some kind of new aid and tried to jump the wall! I felt, I positively felt, Natalie's eyes popping out of their sockets.

I turned my head and said, "Er – this is Jason, Nat. We met at the new saddlers."

"When – this morning?" The incredulity in her voice was as clear as the why – didn't – you – TELL – me in her eyes.

"Mm," I turned back to him. "Did you get the job?"

His face fell, "No. He's not taking on any staff at the moment. He's going to wait and see how busy he gets."

"Jason likes horses," I explained to Natalie, "so he asked for a job involved with saddlery."

"Why on earth do you want to work there?" Nat had slid off Rio's back and pulled her hat off, tousling her blonde hair prettily. "The owner seems a real misery. I bet he won't pay much anyway. If you like horses you should get a job working in a stables."

Jason scowled. I was glad he wasn't impressed by her hair.

"I don't ride," he said and looked back at me. "You're really good Kate. I don't know what you were doing but it looked perfect to me."

Natalie flushed, suddenly realising what a clown she must have looked on Rio.

I said quickly, "Amber – that's this pony, makes it look very easy. Natalie's horse is the one that really takes the riding."

He looked at her and the chestnut mare somewhat coolly. "If you say so. Anyway, sorry to interrupt, but I spotted your card as I left the shop and thought I ought to come over."

"The one with our advert on?" Natalie loosened Rio's girth and tried another smile at him. "You're thinking of learning to ride then? Good. My mother's the best ..."

"Not that one." He obviously hadn't forgiven her for the comment about "morons who knew nothing about horses" in the shop. "It's the other one, Kate. The one about the horse you found."

"Runaway?" I hopped off Amber and started leading her towards the yard. "Come on round while we untack them. The stray horse is there too. D'you know where he comes from then?"

For one delirious moment I thought he might say HE owned the bay horse. I pictured him saying, "My horse has taken to you so strongly I'd like you to come over to my place and ride out with me every day." Jason must have knocked my brains out as well as my breathing when he bumped into me!

"Unfortunately not," was what he actually said, "but he sounds like a horse I saw someone having trouble with yesterday."

"Take a look and see." I pointed to the end stable.

Runaway was looking out at the yard with interest and he whickered a friendly greeting when we came into sight. Jason was still on his bike, pedalling slowly alongside me.

"Leave your bike here." I swiftly untacked my pony and put her anti-sweat rug on. "I'll leave Amber to cool down and come over with you. The stray horse is just a bit nervous though he's already settling down."

Jason propped the bike against the wall. I noticed he was limping and wondered vaguely what he'd done to his leg.

"Here he is." I stroked Runaway's velvet nose and he nuzzled me affectionately in return.

"That's him," Jason's voice was positive. "He wasn't quiet like this though – he was pulling this bloke all over the place and making a heck of a noise. That's what made me stop and look."

"Where was this?" Natalie joined us and I saw Jason's face darken.

"About a mile or so from here," he replied shortly.

"In a stable, field, where?" Natalie couldn't understand his chilly treatment of her. "And why are you so sure it was this horse?"

"Because of this." Jason touched the white mark on Runaway's nose. His movements were calm and the horse sniffed his palm briefly, not at all alarmed. "I was quite close to the lorry that was parked at the side of the road and when – Runaway – started his rumpus I could see him clearly. I remember thinking this mark was unusual, like a perfect crescent moon. It's called a snip isn't it?"

"That's right." For someone who knew nothing about horses I thought he was doing really well. "But what was happening, Jason? Was someone trying to load the horse into the lorry?"

"Not when I saw them. I think the horsebox must have broken down, or had a flat tyre maybe. It had pulled in at the side of Wheelers Lane and a couple of men were bringing the horses out. Two were tied to the box itself and one of the blokes was trying to tie this one up as well. But the horse wasn't having any – were you, Runaway?"

The bay horse blew down his nose as if verifying the story and I scratched his neck absently. "But why ..."

"D'you want to ride down there? It might make more sense to you if you see exactly where." Jason still had his back half turned to Natalie and was talking just to me. "There are a few houses further along Wheelers Lane, maybe someone there will know more about it."

"Good idea." I looked at Natalie. "Shall I tack Amber up again?"

"I think JASON," she said his name very sarkily, obviously not pleased at the way he was ignoring her, "meant we should ride there on bicycles. Didn't you, JASON?"

He shrugged. "Whatever you like. But if you're going to take that horse of yours maybe you should rig it up with a safety net first. You seem to have trouble staying aboard."

"Oooh nasty" I thought, but couldn't help grinning.

Natalie drew in her breath and turned sharply away. "You can talk," she muttered. "Falling off a horse occasionally is inevitable, but what happened to your leg – tumble off your BMX did you?"

I'm used to all the teasing that goes on at Falconhurst but I could see Jason didn't find her retort at all funny. He actually went quite white and I thought the best thing was to separate him and Nat pretty darn quick.

"Come on." I touched his arm gently and felt a definite tingle. "You're right, it'll be quicker by bike. Mine's just round the corner from yours."

He limped across the yard with me and I pedalled down the drive behind him, legs going like little pistons trying to keep up.

"Jason," I yelled, as he started to disappear up

the lane, "wait for me!"

He slowed down immediately and we rode to the main road, then across it and along another quiet, leafy lane similar to the one where Falconhurst stands.

"I don't come this way often," I said as we cycled along. "The bit of open common we use for hacking is in the opposite direction."

"This used to be a real country lane." His good-looking face was still a bit grim, I thought. "But they've built on it quite a lot and with the main road just at the end it's become part of the town now."

"It's the same with the riding school," I began. "Oh, is this it?"

Jason had pulled onto the grass verge and was looking at the ground, still sitting astride the bike. I got off mine and put it down.

"Really deep tyre marks," I said. "It was a big horsebox then, obviously."

"Enormous," he scraped at the mud with his toe. "One of those you see at big shows – they carry five or six, don't they?"

I thought how keen on horses he must be to go along to the shows and said, "Yes they do. Oh look, hoofprints."

Jason got off the bike and limped over. "There should be at least three lots, there might have been more horses still to be unloaded. I think Runaway was further back when I saw him. I'd just passed the lorry and was turning to look at the horses when I saw him pulling against the rope one of the men had hold of. He was making a racket about it as I said, and I stopped for a minute in case he was hurt."

"Did the men say anything?" I was trying to trace the muddle of prints that he thought were the bay horse's.

"I couldn't repeat it." There was a shade of a grin on his face. "He was swearing and cussing at your Runaway and when I called out he turned his head and gave me a real mouthful as well."

"Sounds a nice sort." I was peering at the ground and frowning. "I thought I'd be able to pick out our boy's prints easily, he's lost a shoe on his near fore, but none of these show one missing."

"I'm sure he was about here. The bloke told me to clear off, or words to that effect, and I biked slowly down that way. I didn't like the way he was handling the horse so I stopped and looked back. He'd managed to tie him to the lorry by then."

"And the horsebox was over there?" I pointed and he nodded.

"Mm. As I say I can only assume it had broken down or something. There'd be no reason to stop and unload here – there are no paddocks or stables in this lane. I was worried the bloke might be tying the horse up so he could punish it, give it a beating, maybe. I rode out of sight and waited a while, but then came back to make sure the horse was all right. The guy had just tied it to the lorry and he and the other man were working on the far side wheel I think."

"Even after he swore at you, you still came back to check?" I looked at him and he flushed slightly.

"Well – um – I was just concerned about the horse. I don't like seeing people get rough with animals and ..." He was quite embarrassed, as if I'd accused him of doing something underhand.

"I think it was brilliant of you," I said warmly and he gave me a sideways grin that made my heart do a pole vault.

I gulped and carried on hoofprint hunting so he wouldn't notice. "Over here," I said. "Up against the lorry's tyre marks there's an absolute maze of prints. One of the horse has been thrashing around all over the place. It must be Runaway."

Jason knelt down for a closer look. "That's right ..." He broke off and started to move back the way we'd come, eyes fixed on the ground.

I followed him, realising he'd found a trail of prints leading away from the horsebox. He stopped and bent down so suddenly I nearly fell over him.

"What did you say about a lost shoe?" He'd picked up something that glinted in the morning sun.

I reached out. "Runaway's!" I took the iron shoe and looked at it. "This proves he was here. You were absolutely right. But what on earth was going on?"

He slid the horseshoe into his pocket and shook his head. "I honestly can't think. My first thought was that they had mechanical trouble and had unloaded the horses so they could do whatever repair was needed. Fair enough, but what was going on with your brown horse? He seemed docile enough at Falconhurst but he was going mad with this bunch when I saw him."

"He's very sweet natured," I agreed. "But any horse will cause a rumpus if he's frightened. It looks as though our Runaway was scared enough to pull himself free and go galloping off – Goodness, that means he went charging straight across the main road!"

"He must have done," Jason agreed. "You found him outside the riding school didn't you?"

I told him about Runaway being in the Gray's garden. He laughed at the bit about Mr Gray bouncing up and down on his lawn and I felt the now familiar tremor run through me at the difference a smile made to his dark face.

"What I really don't understand" we were walking back for our bikes, "is why no one reported losing the horse to the police. It was yesterday evening when you saw the lorry here. Is that right?"

"Yes." Jason was still limping I noticed. "It was just getting dark – about nineish I think."

"Nine o'clock," I said thoughtfully. "It was one in the morning when the police phoned Sandra about the straying horse. Four hours later. Assuming the horsebox HAD broken down and they took that long to fix it, why would the two men carefully reload it, then drive off leaving one extremely valuable member of their cargo galloping around the country?"

"Doesn't make sense," Jason agreed. "How do you know the brown – I mean the bay – horse is valuable?"

"He looks wonderful," I said absently. "Anyway Sandra says so."

"Oh, the know-all mother of the know-all Natalie." His scowl was back in place.

"She IS pretty terrific actually," I said, a little severely. "And in fact I agree with Nat, you ought to go to Falconhurst for riding lessons. You'd be ..."

"I'd be blowed if I would." He yanked his bike off the ground and flung himself on it. "I thought you were OK, Kate, but you're just another mickey taker aren't you?"

And to my utter dismay he spun the bike round and rode rapidly away, leaving me gaping, open mouthed by the roadside.

CHAPTER FOUR

"I THINK HE'S JUST bad tempered and moody." Natalie tossed her blonde head and perched cross legged on a straw bale. "He was quite foul to me, I thought."

"I told you!" I felt near to tears after describing how Jason had dumped me. "That was because you made all those remarks about morons who knew nothing about horses, while we were at the saddlers."

"Well, OK, but I was perfectly friendly when he turned up here." Natalie fluffed up her hair. "He made it quite clear he wanted nothing to do with me, insulted me AND my horse, then got all stroppy when I made a little joke about him falling off his bike. What has he done to his leg anyway?"

"I don't know," I admitted. "I don't know anything at all about him. All I can tell is that he's kind, because he worried when he thought someone was going to hurt an animal. And he's interested enough in horses to ride over here with news of our stray one."

"Maybe it wasn't interest in horses that made him call in at Falconhurst." Nat grinned at me slyly. "You two seemed to get on very well after your crashing meeting."

"We did." I pretended not to know what she

meant. "We were both very concerned about Runaway."

"It's OK, Kate," she winked knowingly. "He IS good looking, I admit. It's a pity he's so nasty and bad tempered."

"But he's not," I wailed, forgetting to act cool. "Jason's warm and kind and – it must have been something I said."

"What must?" Sandra put her head round the barn door. "Lunch time, you two. Monkey says someone came asking about Runaway. A lad on a bike."

"No, no, Mum, it was a knight on a white charger." Natalie threw some straw at me, but I was so depressed I just shook my head sadly.

"Look at your hair!" Sandra ruffled it, sending dusty fronds flying. "It always looks so beautiful when you arrive, Kate. What will your mother think?"

I didn't care, and said so. I did care what Jason had thought of it, but I didn't say that.

"So!" Sandra put a big bowl of salad on the kitchen table and we sat down. "What did this young man say about our stray horse then? And no teasing from you, Natalie. Your tongue's a bit too sharp for my liking today."

"Ooh!" Natalie went pink with indignation but she left me alone, thank goodness.

"He recognised the description you put on your

card." I helped myself to salad. "He doesn't know much about horses, he said, but he was quite definite he'd seen Runaway." I quickly told her how Jason had shown me the horsebox tracks and the hoofprints.

"And he's quite sure it's the same horse?" Sandra sounded doubtful. "One bay horse looks very much like another to an inexperienced eye."

"Jason's positive," I said. "He remembers thinking the snip on the horse's nose was like a crescent moon. And it is."

"It is indeed. It's just – well the story doesn't make sense. Presuming the horsebox had broken down, why would the men work on it then drive off without one of the horses? I think Jason must be mistaken. The horsebox episode must be just a coincidence. Our stray must be from somewhere else – somewhere local ..."

"The shoe!" I remembered suddenly. "We traced a set of hoofprints leading away from the box and Jason actually found the shoe our stray had thrown. That proves it was Runaway."

"Good grief!" Sandra stared at me. "I suppose it must do. Have you got it, Kate? We could compare it as a double check."

"No," I admitted. "Jason put it in his pocket."

"Ring him up then and get him to bring it round."

"I can't!" I felt like crying again. "I don't know

what I said but he got mad and just went off. I don't even know his surname, let alone where he lives."

"It's a shame." Natalie was still making little digs. "Jason could have come round here like Prince Charming with the glass slipper, 'Whosoever this horseshoe fits ...'"

"Natalie," her mother said crossly. "Will you stop it. From the sound of it you stirred up trouble with this Jason right from the start."

"I keep telling you he's just moody." Natalie pushed her lunch sulkily around her plate. "I was just joking about his leg ..."

"What's the matter with his leg?" Sandra looked at me.

"I don't know," I said weakly. "He limps. But he can ride a bike all right."

"Maybe he thinks he CAN'T ride a horse," Sandra said thoughtfully. "If he walks with a limp and is sensitive about it he'd hate you two crashing in with your remarks about horse riding."

"We didn't crash – " I began. "At least I don't think we did."

"I hope not. I also hope he gets over whatever it was that upset him. I need to know if our stray horse definitely came from that lorry. Like me, the police are assuming someone from round here will report to them that their horse is missing. If the runaway horse came from further afield I need to let our police station know."

"Of course." Natalie finished her lunch and carried her plate to the sink. "The local police will have to circulate his description all over the country, won't they? Runaway could have come from anywhere."

"I wonder if Jason noticed the lorry's number plate." I thumped the table in frustration. "Oh why didn't I ask his name?"

"You were too busy gazing into his big brown eyes." Natalie was asking for trouble.

"I've warned you!" Sandra glared really fiercely at her tormenting daughter. "Leave Kate alone, can't you see when someone's upset?"

"Sorry Kate." Natalie gave me a sudden hug and I grinned maliciously at her.

"It's all right, Nat. I know you're only keeping on because you're jealous he liked me more than you. Some of us have got it and some of us haven't."

"That's the girl, Kate." Sandra hooted with laughter. "Give her some back! But seriously, how are we going to track the elusive Jason down?"

I got up and started to help with the wiping up. "I honestly don't know, he didn't mention his school or his street or anything ..." I stopped in mid wipe. "But – he asked at the saddlers for a job, didn't he? He'd have given the owner his name and address surely?"

"Brilliant. I'll phone the man." Sandra grabbed the wall phone.

Natalie and I carried on with the clearing up. She'd put washing up foam on her eyebrows and was doing an impression of our science teacher, making me fall about laughing.

We were still giggling when Sandra put the phone down and said, "Got it. An address, anyway, no phone number. I've got time to dash round there now before my afternoon lessons start. Are you two coming?"

We looked at each other and I shook my head. "Not me. I wouldn't know what to say." And my hair still needs washing, I might have added.

"And there's no point in me going." Natalie gave herself a foam beard and smiled sweetly at us both. "For some reason Jason doesn't like the look of me. Can't think why."

"Maybe he'd think you're prettier with whiskers." Sandra put a great dollop on her daughter's nose and moved quickly to the back door.

"Don't you dare start a water fight," she warned, seeing Nat geared up to throw some at her. "I'm off to track down Jason and the Missing Shoe. You two behave yourselves for once."

"Charming." Natalie waved her goodbye from the window. "What shall we do till we're needed in the yard, Kate?"

I was torn between smartening myself up with a quick shower, and seeing how the stray horse was doing. The horse won.

"I think I'll keep Runaway company," I said. "He likes looking out at the yard, I know, but they get bored cooped up in a stable all day. I'll take the radio in and sing to him while I give him a good grooming."

"Oh, lucky, lucky horse. Hang on, I'll just get my ear plugs and I'll come with you." She's such a comedian, isn't she.

We were both in Runaway's loose box, singing and brushing away when Sandra drove back into the yard. She came straight over to us, holding something in her hand.

"It's the shoe," I said, thinking Nat was right and it did sound like an offbeat Cinderella story.

Sandra lifted the bay horse's near fore and held the shoe to it and we could all see it would fit exactly. She then looked at the off fore and compared the shoe on that one.

"There's no doubt about it." She patted Runaway's sleek shoulder. "This is definitely the horse Jason saw the man struggling with in Wheelers Lane. It just doesn't make sense."

"Maybe my original feeling was right." I stopped brushing the horse's thick, dark tail. "Perhaps Runaway has been stolen. If the two men were horse thieves, transporting stolen animals from one part of the country to another, they certainly wouldn't dare tell the police if one got away from them on the way."

"You could be right," Sandra said slowly. "There's still no phone call from anyone whose horse has simply strayed."

"And it would explain why Runaway had a full lead rope on when he wandered into the Grays' garden," I went on. "I KNEW there was something about that rope."

"Well, I'll certainly pass all this on to the police." Sandra unbolted the door. "If it's going to take a while to sort out your Runaway's ownership we'd better turn him out in one of the small paddocks. He's going to get bored stuck in here and he's making short work of my hay supplies too. Come on over with me a minute, Kate, while I phone the police station."

"OK." I followed her, slightly puzzled. As we reached the house I turned and saw Natalie leading Runaway out of the stable. "Hang on, Nat," I called. "Can I take him to the field in a minute?"

"Oh sure," she yelled back good naturedly. "I'll just tie him up outside while I clean the box out, then."

I kicked my boots off and followed Sandra into the kitchen.

"I just wanted a quick word without Natalie

putting her oar in and teasing you all the time," she said. "I only spoke to Jason for a few minutes, but from what he said I think you should go back there and talk to him too."

"Why?" I felt my heart lurch just at the thought. "He stomped off in a total rage this morning. He wouldn't want to see me again would he?"

"I think he would." Sandra patted my shoulder. "He liked you. I could tell that and I think that's why he was so upset when he thought you were making fun of him."

"But I wasn't." I racked my brains to think what I could have said. "I thought it was great the way he went back to make sure the bloke wasn't hurting Runaway. Jason's so interested in horses, I said he should come here and learn to ride."

"That's it then." Sandra sat on the edge of the table and looked at me. "And that's why he was so touchy with Natalie. Lord knows she's not known for her tact, but it was you who really got to him. He thought you were making wisecracks about riding because he's disabled."

"He's not – " I stopped. "The limping? He hasn't just twisted an ankle or something then?"

"No. I met his mother briefly. Not my kind of person, rather fussy and overprotective. When I explained I wanted to see Jason she launched straight into his life story. Apparently they didn't think he'd ever walk, and he's never been able to run or play sport. I think he's quite bitter about it and that makes him – a little oversensitive maybe."

"Oh poor Jason." I felt my eyes fill with tears. "I wasn't making fun, I think he's just brilliant."

"I liked him too." Sandra stood up and reached for the phone "And what's more I'm sure I could teach him to ride if he'd let me. So that's another reason for you going to see him."

She dialled the police station number and told them the latest developments on Runaway's story.

"The sergeant's asking if our witnesses could supply any details about the other horses and the type of lorry." She put a hand over the receiver and hissed at me. "I'll tell him you and Jason will call in and discuss it, shall I?"

"Yes – no – oh heck!" I squealed and heard her say politely, "Thank you sergeant. Jason Brookham and Kate Harvey will come in later. And you'll let me know if you hear – thank you. Goodbye."

She put the phone back and I immediately wailed, "I can't go to his house! What can I say – what – "

"Ssh," Sandra put a finger to my lips. "I can hear someone else yelling. It's Natalie!"

We flew to the kitchen door and dashed outside. Coming towards us at a nice, spanking trot was Runaway, head high and lead rope dangling.

Behind him panted Natalie, still shouting. I stepped forward and the bay horse stopped immediately, again dropping his soft nose into my palm.

"Did he break away from you, Nat?" Sandra looked at her daughter in surprise. Natalie's been around horses for literally all of her fifteen years and can handle them as well as some people and a great deal better than most.

"No, of course not. I tied him up in the yard like I said and threw the bed up." Natalie was panting from the running. "I came out with the barrow and noticed he was fiddling with the quick release knot but I thought he was just chewing at it."

"And?" Sandra was examining the lead rope with interest.

"And – he wasn't chewing it at all – the little devil was undoing it! I dumped the barrow and was walking back. I saw him worrying at the knot again, then he stepped back and the rope just slid through and he was free."

I laughed out loud at her outraged face and gave the bay horse a very undeserved kiss. "So that solves another part of the puzzle doesn't it? Now we know how he got away from the lorry he was tied to. He simply untied the rope and shoved off! Neat trick, Runaway you old rascal."

"A very bright horse, this." Sandra tickled the white crescent on his nose. "Someone must be missing you, mustn't they? Put him in the side paddock, Kate, and let's just hope he can't open gates as well!"

I led the horse back through the yard and into the nice shady paddock at the other end. He stood beautifully while I took his head collar off, then wheeled and pivoted across the grass, kicking up his heels with joy at being out. He had a wonderful action, well balanced and supple, and the curve of his neck showed power and breeding. Natalie and I sat on the gate and watched him roll ecstatically, legs waving vigorously and three shoes glinting in the sun.

"Touch of the old love at first sight for you, isn't it?" She grinned in her usual wicked way at me and I felt my face go hot again.

"What d'you – Oh you mean Runaway? He is lovely isn't he, but I'm not letting myself forget he belongs to someone else."

"As long as you don't ,or you'll end up getting hurt." She slid off the gate and started walking back. "I've got to give a hand with the next class."

I gave one last, lingering look at the now peacefully grazing horse and followed her.

"Are you helping too?" She asked over her shoulder.

"I won't if you don't mind. I – er – think I'll take a shower." I walked quickly on towards the house and pretended I couldn't hear her questions.

As I opened the kitchen door I distinctly heard her call out to Monkey, "What's Kate up to? A shower! In the middle of the day I ask you! A shower!"

CHAPTER FIVE

I FELT A LOT BETTER for it. I used some lovely zingy grapefruit shampoo and even bothered with conditioner on the ends of my thick brown hair. It's naturally curly and the longer it gets the wilder it looks. My mum used to cut it very short to keep me tidy, and I've always hated it but the bigger and shaggier I let it get the more I like it. I wavered a bit about what to wear. I had one decent top with me and some newish cotton chinos but I decided they'd look too dressed up. In the end I pulled on my beloved old jeans with the rip in the knee and a baggy tee shirt.

I peeked in the hall mirror and thought I looked quite good. If I was just a bit taller Jason might – I shook myself. I was only going there to convince him I hadn't been making fun of him, that I really did think Sandra could get him riding a horse and that I'd like him to accompany me to the police station. Put like that it sounded ridiculous and I thought I'd better rehearse what to say on my way over to his house.

I sneaked my bike past the yard and pedalled off before Natalie could spot me and ask just where I was going. I rode along the lane, going as fast as I could past the Grays' house, and arrived at the neat estate where Jason lived about twenty minutes later.

I pushed my bike up the drive and took a deep breath. I'd practised this really good speech, including a few polite words introducing myself to his mother. I was quite sure she'd answer the door and I'd have to work hard at being charming before she'd even let me see her son.

And that was assuming her son would want to see me anyway. I felt very, very nervous. I ran my tongue over lips so dry they felt like paper, and rang the door bell. I waited, saying under my breath, "Good afternoon, Mrs Brookham," and wondering whether I'd be expected to shake hands. After a couple of minutes I rang the bell again and still the dragon of a mother didn't appear. I couldn't believe after all this build-up there was no one in. I rang once more and was just about to turn away when a window above me opened and Jason stuck his head out.

"Who – Oh it's you! I don't suppose you know anything about parrots do you?"

I gaped up at him, careful speech forgotten. "I – ah – well, yes a bit actually." (My Gran's had one for years. We've got a photo of it perched on the side of my cot looking in at the baby.)

"Brilliant!" Jason's dark face broke into a welcoming grin. "Trouble is I don't know how to let you in."

I caught on very quickly. "You've got a parrot

flying loose in the house?"

"Yes," he scratched his head. "It's swooping about in the hall and landing. I've shut the door to this room, so I could open the window but – "

I stepped back so I could see him better. "Close that window. Nip out of the room, down the stairs and into the kitchen, closing THAT door behind you. Then I can come in through the back without the parrot escaping."

"Brilliant," he said again and disappeared.

I walked round to the back of the house and waited. I heard the sound of doors opening and shutting, then the back door was flung wide and there was Jason. He looked hot and dishevelled.

"I've been going mad with this ruddy bird," he drew me into the kitchen and shut the door firmly behind me. "My mother's looking after it for someone while they're on holiday. I felt sorry for it cooped up in its cage so I let it out for a little fly round when she went out."

"And now you can't get it back in." I grinned at him, and he smiled back, the wonderful dark eyes looking deep into mine. I felt the knees start to go and pulled myself together with an effort. "OK. What kind is it? Is it hand tame, do you know?"

"Kind?" He ran a hand wildly through his hair. "It's a big grey thing. And it's not showing tameness of any sort."

"It's probably an African grey, then," I said

54

knowledgeably. "Same as my Gran's. Where is he now?"

"He was perched on the top banister," Jason said grimly. "Amongst a thousand other places. But as I came down the stairs to you he flew past me and into the living room. So I shut him in there."

"That's good." We walked into the hall. "Is that where his cage is?"

"Yup. I thought when I let him out I could just wave my arms around a bit and he'd go back in. But whenever I get near him he sort of hisses and takes off in the opposite direction."

He opened a door very gingerly and said, "In here. How do we get in without letting him out?"

I peeped past him. "He's on the curtain rail at the far end. We'll sneak in without opening the door wide."

I slid past him and into the room. It was full of pretty furniture and dinky ornaments. Not the ideal place to have a parrot flying free.

"What's his name?" I whispered to Jason as he edged in behind me and clicked the door shut.

"Alexander," he said, looking exasperatedly towards the still perching parrot. "As in 'The Great'. It's not what I've been calling him for the past half-hour, I can tell you. He's broken one of my mother's figurines and nibbled a chunk out of the picture rail. She's going to kill me."

I suppressed a giggle and walked towards the window. The big cage was to the right of it, just underneath the red and grey bird.

"Alexander," I crooned. "What a clever boy. Come to Kate then."

The parrot raised his crest and looked down at me. I held out some sunflower seeds I'd taken from his feed dish.

"Clever boy. Pretty boy."

"Pretty boy," he repeated and I heard Jason give a quiet groan.

I stayed quite still with my arm stretched out, the seeds lying in the flat of my palm. Alexander muttered and walked jerkily along the curtain rail, still looking down at me.

I kept talking to him quietly until he suddenly flew down and perched on my wrist, picking up a sunflower seed from my hand in his great curved beak.

"Clever, clever boy." I scratched his head and he raised and lowered the crest in pleasure.

Jason had stayed rooted to the spot. He watched in amazement as I walked to the cage and put my hand inside it. Alexander sidled along my wrist and hopped peacefully onto the perch. I closed the cage door securely and turned back to Jason, trying hard not to look smug.

"I don't believe it." He put his arms out as if to hug me. "Just like that! If you knew the trouble

I've had!"

"He's probably scared of you. I expect he belongs to a woman, that's why he came to me so easily."

"Whatever the reason, I can't tell you how pleased I am to see you." He'd put his arms back down, to my disappointment.

"And me to see you." I gave a silent vote of thanks to the flyaway parrot for breaking the ice so well, and decided to plunge straight in. "I'm sorry you thought I was taking the mickey this morning. I wasn't."

He looked embarrassed. "It's me who's sorry. It's about time I stopped being so touchy. I thought – I thought you were really nice, so when you started making cracks about horse riding I was upset you seemed as bad as your cocky friend."

"Neither of us are bad really." I felt a distinct glow because he'd thought I was nice. "We assumed you were limping because you'd hurt your ankle, maybe. We fall off the horses so often one of us is usually hobbling or one handed."

He was swiftly tidying up a few of the knocked over ornaments. "You're very direct anyway." His voice was gruff. "People usually pretend they haven't noticed anything wrong with me unless they're the kind to make fun. It was worse when I was in a wheelchair. Then everyone assumed I was mentally defective as well as crippled."

"It's good you're neither then, isn't it?" As he was looking so self-conscious I decided to change the subject. "Because we need your help again, if you would. Can you spare an hour or so now?"

"Sure." His dark, wary face was lit by another fabulous smile. "But what can I do?"

"Come to the police station with me." I explained about Runaway undoing his rope in the yard. "So Sandra thinks I might be right about him being stolen. And the police would like to know if you can remember anything else that could help them trace the horsebox."

"Aw heck, why didn't I take its number?" He groaned. "It didn't occur to me that Runaway and the others might be stolen. I thought the guy moving them was a rough so and so, that's all."

"We still don't know for sure what the story is." I was walking with Jason to collect his bike from the garage. His arm was so close I could feel the warmth from it and the sensation made me feel almost dizzy.

"You OK?" He seemed aware my head was spinning and his dark eyes were full of concern. "Are you worrying about your stray horse – Runaway?"

"Yes, I suppose I am. I like all horses but – I don't know why – this one and I seemed to hit it off straight away. It usually takes a long time to establish trust but we seem to know each other already."

"I know how Runaway feels," he said unexpectedly. "There's something about you, Kate, a gentleness, kindness, something lovely. Even Alexander felt it! I guess that's why I was so upset when – "

"When you thought I was making fun." I tried to lighten the air by grinning at him cheekily. "And as for being kind and gentle – I'm known as Knockout Kate, I've got such a temper."

"You're a knockout all right," he touched my hair, quite shyly. "Even with all that grass in this lot I thought so."

I felt like you do on one of those space rides at the fair. Excited and exhilarated with a spinning head and a slightly sicky tum. It was all going too fast for me. I got on my bike and rode off, not looking back at Jason at all. I just hoped he was following and that he wouldn't say anything else as embarrassingly nice – well not in front of Natalie anyway. I usually tell her everything that happens to me but I could just picture her face at the news that someone liked me that much that quickly.

To my relief Jason was back to his usual slightly guarded self when we got to the station.

"I don't think I'm going to be any help," he said as we went in. "The other two horses I saw were ordinary, as far as I can remember."

The sergeant greeted us cheerfully and said there was still no report of any local horse gone missing.

"So we must assume your detective work is correct and the horse was being transported into our area in the horsebox seen by you – er – Jason."

"Definitely," we both said together and our eyes met in amusement.

"We matched the shoe from Wheelers Lane against the three on Runaway – the lost, or I suppose you'd call him the found horse," I said. "But I think Sandra told you that."

"Yes she did." The sergeant looked at his notes. "We need to tie in the horsebox now, find out where it came from and so on. If the horses were being transported for legitimate purposes – i.e. they were not stolen – we have to inform the lorry driver he's lost one."

"He'd know that by now," I said impatiently. "If, for some crazy reason, the men didn't realise the bay horse had got away last night, they'd certainly have noticed they were one horse short when they came to unload them, surely?"

"Surely," the big policeman echoed solemnly and I saw Jason's lips twitch into a smile. "Bear with me, Miss, while I get some details from the young man here. Jason, isn't it?"

"Yes. I've been racking my brains and I can't think of anything that will help. It was a big, modern horsebox, but I'm afraid I didn't make a note of its number plate. I was looking at Runaway you see – the horse Kate rescued I mean. He was whinnying and stamping about, looking upset. I was quite close to him, that's when I noticed the snip, the mark on his nose."

"I see. And the men themselves? Were you near enough to be able to give me a description of them?"

Jason shook his head, looking rueful. "Nothing that helps. The one holding onto the horse's rope was average height and thin. He had a cap on with the peak pulled down low so I didn't get a really good look at his face. I only saw the back of the other man – he was heavier and might have been older but I can't really say."

The sergeant was writing all this down. "And there were two other horses tied to the lorry as well? What were they like?"

Poor Jason scratched his head. "About the same size as the bay one. One was darker with a longer mane and tail I think and the other one was just an ordinary brownish one. Sorry, I'm not an expert like Kate here, she'd have been able to tell you exactly what they were like."

"Not to worry," the sergeant said soothingly. "You're doing better than me. A horse would have to be covered in pink polka dots for me to identify it. Now, back to the lorry. Was there anything –

anything at all?"

Jason screwed his eyes shut, obviously going back in his mind, picturing the scene as he'd turned into Wheelers Lane and heard the commotion Runaway was making.

"It was a light colour, white or maybe cream," he said slowly.

"Was there any writing on the side?" I asked eagerly, realising he was recalling the picture.

"I can't – no – hang on." He opened his eyes and looked straight at me. "There was a shape in dark red – a circle? No a diamond, a big diamond."

"Oh well done, Jason." I nearly flung my arms round him but caught myself just in time. "That's just what we needed, isn't it, Sergeant?"

"Is it? Yes, I suppose it IS, in that it will make the lorry more easily identified, but it will still take quite a time to get the description circulated and – "

"No, no!" I was dancing up and down in excitement. "A diamond, a big red diamond – don't you know what that means?"

Both he and Jason looked at me as if I'd lost my marbles. They looked so comical I started laughing, tried to disguise it into a cough and ended up choking and spluttering. Jason thumped my back and the sergeant fetched me a glass of water. After a few sips and a bit more coughing I calmed down again.

"You were saying?" Jason said in exaggeratedly

polite tones, raising his eyebrows wickedly.

"Don't set me off again," I warned. "I was saying the sign on the side of the lorry tells us where the horsebox came from – the Diamond Stud!"

"Sounds like a cuff link." The policeman was writing it down anyway. "But it's obviously somewhere important in the horsey world, is that right?"

"That's right," I said reverently. "The Diamond Centre is just about the biggest and most prestigious equestrian setup in the country. They're breeders of course, but they have dressage and showjumping and cross-country, three-day eventing – oh you name it!"

"And where is it?" The sergeant's hand hovered over the phone. "I'll ring them now."

My face fell. "I don't know the address. It's north of here – maybe the Midlands – sorry, I've never been there, a bit up-market for me."

"I'll run it through our computer," he said. "That'll give me the lowdown. Then we can find out from the Diamond Centre direct just what their lorry was doing in Wheelers Lane last night."

"And why their men drove off and left a horse," I said. "No wonder Runaway looks so terrific, Jason. If he's from the Diamond – "

"Whew." Jason grinned at me and my heart did its usual gymnastic routine. "Is whew the right thing to say?"

"Quite right," I said. "Shall we sit down over there while the sergeant does his investigating?"

"OK." He limped over and sank down in a chair.

"Does your leg hurt?" I asked and watched his dark face become immediately shuttered.

"A bit," he said shortly.

I sighed. "Oh come on. I'm your mate, all right? You can tell me. Does it hurt too much to ride a horse, for instance?"

He glared at me for a moment, then relaxed when he realised I really wanted to know.

"How can I tell? I was told I'd never walk, but I do, then I was told I couldn't ride a bike but I can. Both hurt, but not enough to stop me."

"Not enough to stop you because you WANT to do them," I said. "So if you want to ride a horse, why not try?"

"Because I'd feel a fool." He said it very honestly. "I've hung round places like Falconhurst. It's always little kids in the beginners' classes. By the time they're eleven or twelve they can ride well enough to go out on their own. I'd feel a right Charlie being towed along the road on the end of a rope behind them."

"You wouldn't have to be," I argued. "Some beginners do get taken out on leading reins I grant you, but you could take lessons in the school till

64

you're proficient enough to hack out. You're big and strong looking – I bet it wouldn't take you long at all."

"And maybe it's impossible for someone like me to learn at all. Riding a bike was OK, I've adapted mine to suit my leg, but you can't adapt a horse can you?"

"They'll be ways of altering the aids, I should think. Look, ask Sandra about it. If she says it's not on, you haven't lost anything have you?"

He muttered something under his breath about "hope" but at that moment the sergeant called us back to the desk so I couldn't ask.

The man was looking quite animated. "I've been in touch," he said. "Well spotted you two, that horsebox did come from the Diamond Centre."

"And they're coming back to pick up their horse?" I felt my voice flatten. I knew I was going to hate losing Runaway.

"No. No, they're not," he looked at us both. "That lorry, horsebox, whatever you like to call it, was stolen from their premises two days ago. There were no horses inside it. They say they pride themselves on the security for their livestock.

"So who – where were Runaway and the others from?" Jason looked at him, bewildered.

"I checked the computer," the sergeant put down his notes triumphantly. "And you can draw a line between the Diamond Centre and here. And on that line in the last day or so there have been at least four horses reported as stolen. You were right, Miss Harvey – your Runaway was running away from a pair of horse thieves!"

CHAPTER SIX

"CLEVER OLD KATE!" Sandra thumped my back. "I thought you were mad sleeping in the stable to guard that horse, but your feeling about him was right."

"You slept in his stable?" Jason was in Falconhurst's kitchen with me, looking slightly uncomfortable and withdrawn again.

"Mm. I thought the baddies might trace Runaway to our yard and have another go at stealing him."

"Kate was going to tackle the gang single handed." Natalie had come rushing in from the yard when she saw us. "She might be only small but she's got a black belt in Origami you know."

"Isn't that Japanese paper folding?" Jason looked confused.

"Ignore her," I said. "Nat can't speak without trying to be funny."

"She rides a horse the same way too, doesn't she?" He smiled innocently at her and she glared back immediately.

Sandra laughed and stepped between them. "No fighting! Natalie, it serves you right, you shouldn't dish out all this teasing if you can't take it yourself."

Her daughter took a deep breath. "OK. But I

warn you, Jason Brookham, as soon as you can ride a horse, Rio and I will gallop you over the heath till you beg for mercy. Kate, Monkey needs a hand with the next class – you coming?"

"Sure." I started to follow her out. "Will you stay and talk some more to Sandra?" I asked Jason.

He looked at her. "If you've time?"

"I've got time," she smiled and I saw him relax.

Natalie and I helped Monkey with a "tiny tots" class, leading the ponies and generally assisting some quite small children having their first lesson. I saw what Jason meant when he talked about the embarrassment factor of being a fully grown learner. After the lesson I took a couple of the little Dartmoor ponies back to their field. It was the one adjoining Runaway's and he cantered over to the fence as soon as he saw us, head high and tail streaming. He looked quite beautiful and I stopped to make a fuss of him and tell him the latest update.

"So you see," I had my arms round his neck, loving the way the muscles rippled under his skin and breathing in the sweet horsey smell of him, "you ARE stolen, but then you knew that. And you were a very clever boy to untie that lead rope and get away from those men. Though how you got across that main road I don't – "

"Maybe he used a zebra crossing." Jason's strong hand tousled Runaway's mane, his fingers briefly touching mine.

I controlled my instantly wobbly knees and smiled at him. "You've caught on fast to the Falconhurst tradition of perpetual teasing."

He gave me a devastating grin. "If you can't beat them join 'em. Sandra doesn't see any reason why I can't learn to ride. I start tomorrow, so I hope you won't mind me being around."

"I won't mind," I said, trying hard not to do cartwheels and shout yippee.

"It's a shame Runaway won't be here too," he added. "I see what you mean about you two liking each other."

"We certainly do." I gave the bay horse a last pat and walked back to the yard with him. "I'd love to ride him before his owner collects him but it's not on I don't suppose."

"Why not? The police will contact them with the news but I bet it'll be tomorrow before they get here. Take him out this afternoon."

"We don't have any tack and it wouldn't be right – " I called out to Natalie and asked her what she thought.

"Mum will say no," she said straight away. "But she's going out later so give him a little spin in the field. You won't hurt him, and anyway if it wasn't for you the owners might not HAVE a horse to collect."

I looked at them both. "D'you think it will be

OK?"

"Course it will." Jason gave me another grin. "Sandra said I could stay around to learn a few chores and pick up some tips on horse care from Monkey. Watching you ride Runaway will be good for me."

"There you are Kate," Natalie said slyly. "You ought to do it just for Jason's sake."

"What are you three up to?" Monkey's wrinkled face was screwed up suspiciously. "Sandra said you were my working party while she's out but I don't see much work being done."

"What can I do to help?" Jason lifted a barrow and limped rapidly towards the stables. "Show me how to muck out, Monkey."

"I'll show you," I said but was shoved aside in the groom's usual friendly fashion.

"You're cleaning tack, Mighty Mouse. And you, Nat. You can gossip away to your heart's content then while we men get on with the real stuff."

"Well!" Natalie and I said indignantly but we went off to the tack room. In the yard Monkey's the boss and we know it.

"He and Jason seem to be getting on well," I remarked, looking out at the yard where they'd finished skipping out the stables. "Nice for Monkey to have another man around the place, I suppose."

Natalie was polishing vigorously. "In fact it's

nice for everyone except me."

"How do you work that one out?"

"Well, Jason likes Monkey, he really, REALLY likes you and he's bound to like Mum once she starts teaching him. But he can't stand me. I'm going to feel like the odd one out."

"Rubbish." I threw a sponge at her. "Jason's already coming round. Remember his first impression of you wasn't too great. You were in a foul mood because of the Grays, stomping about and calling everyone names. He'll soon find out what a good-natured old softie you are really."

"Thanks pal." She picked up the sponge and threw it back. "And no doubt he'll also discover what a dreadful temper his sweet and pretty little Kate has."

"Who, me?" I gazed at her all wide eyed and innocent.

"Oh, look, the two MEN are going off somewhere." Natalie jumped to her feet. "Shall we sort out a saddle for Runaway while Monkey's out of the yard? I'm sure Rio's will fit him. We'll put a thick padded numnah under it. You'll only be aboard for a few minutes so it won't do him any harm."

"Good!" I was starting to feel quite nervous about this trial ride. The bay horse was sweet natured and seemed very well behaved but he was obviously capable of playing up as Jason had already witnessed.

I couldn't say any of this to my friend of course. Natalie's been riding since she was scarcely more than a baby and it wouldn't occur to her to be worried about it. We sneaked the tack across to Runaway's paddock. He was still contentedly grazing but he raised his head and whickered a greeting at me.

"Amazing," Nat commented. "I've had Rio for nearly a year and she still doesn't do that for me."

I grinned and hoped the bay horse would be as friendly when I rode him. We'd gone back to our tack cleaning when Monkey and Jason came back into the yard. They'd been to fetch Sable, Falconhurst's oldest working horse, who's about twenty-five.

"Still as full of wickedness as ever though." I could hear Monkey grumbling. "You did a good job of catching him, young Jason. The last time I needed him it took three of us twenty minutes to corner the old devil."

"Doesn't he like work then?" Jason was scratching the old horse between his ears while watching intently everything the groom did.

"He doesn't mind it at all. The little bit we get him to do just keeps life interesting for him. It's just a habit some horses get into and no matter what you do they always stay difficult. I'll show you how to pick his feet out now – "

I smiled at the picture they made – the young, good-ooking Jason concentrating completely on the much older and definitely less attractive twosome of Monkey and Sable.

"He's really enjoying it," I said and Natalie pretended not to know who I meant.

"Who can you be talking about, Kate? If you're thinking of carrying Sable's tack over to him you'd better wipe that soppy look off your face. It's a dead giveaway."

I socked her with the sponge again and let Jason fetch it himself, just in case she was right. Once they'd tacked the horse up, Monkey led him behind the yard to the schooling ring to meet his pupil. Jason swept and tidied up then limped a little uncertainly towards the tack room.

"I can't go with him." He gave me that devastating shy smile. "The lady he's teaching is quite nervous and doesn't like anyone else around when she has her lessons. I can sympathise with that so is it all right if I watch you try Runaway out, Kate?"

"Course," I said, with a confidence I didn't feel. "I'm only going to sit on him and take him round the field a couple of times. Not much excitement I'm afraid."

"You never know," Natalie said happily. "He could be a real bucking bronco of a horse couldn't he – clever enough to undo knots so who knows what he's capable of under saddle?"

"Thanks a lot," I said, and stuffed my clean and bouncing hair into a skull cap.

I called Runaway over to the gate and Nat held him while I gently slid the saddle in place. "You were right – it's a pretty good fit. How about the bridle?" I asked her.

"OK. I just need to lengthen the cheek pieces. The bit's fine though."

I tightened the girth, pulled down the stirrup irons and prepared to mount. My heart was hammering almost as loudly as when Jason had bowled me over. I took a deep breath and sprang lightly into the saddle. Runaway stood stock still, the very model of a well-schooled horse. I asked him to walk on and he moved away immediately, covering the soft springy turf in a free-moving pace. He felt wonderful, his neck curving gently, his back and loins supple as he accepted the bit. We walked the long length of the paddock and across the top, then back towards the gate. I asked for trot and the working tempo he produced was just perfect. I rode past Natalie and Jason watching intently at the gate and I honestly didn't notice them, I was concentrating so much and enjoying myself hugely.

Once more round the field and I was heading for the gate again. "I'll stop now," I yelled. "He's wonderful, absolutely perfect."

"Let's see him canter then," Natalie called back

and I sat for a couple of strides and nudged behind the girth with my outside leg.

Runaway flowed into a beautifully united tempo and we cantered at a nicely balanced, controlled pace to rejoin our two spectators.

"You should see your face!" Nat greeted me. "I've never seen such a big soppy grin. Oh I don't know, perhaps I have – "

"Shut up, you," I said quickly, scared she was going to embarrass me. "Isn't he LOVELY?"

"You two look great together." Jason was smiling in flattering admiration.

"It's a terrible shame he's not going to be around long." I hopped off and hugged the bay horse, hiding my face in his mane. "I just hope whoever owns him loves him as much as he deserves."

"Course they do." Nat helped me swiftly untack. "He's so well trained and very fit looking, that shows he's had a lot of time spent on him. Don't go all mooney eyed about the horse, Kate."

"No, I won't," I said, trying hard not to. "But he really is – "

"I know, I know, LOVELY!" Natalie sang out, pulling a sarky face and I saw Jason scowl.

We sneaked Rio's tack back to the yard and were all diligently polishing away when Monkey came back with a refreshed looking Sable.

"Three wise monkeys, you are." He looked at us

with suspicion. "See no evil, hear no evil, speak no evil. You've been up to something."

"How can you SAY that?" I jumped up and put my hat back on. "Please can I ride Sable back to his field? You don't mind, do you Nat?"

"Ride away," she yawned lazily. "I got fed up years ago with all that sort of stuff."

"Can I come with you?" Jason had carefully untacked the cob under Monkey's supervision, and was fastening the head collar buckle.

"Sure you can," I said. "It won't be very interesting for you though."

"I'll show you how to give a leg up." Monkey winked at him. "Watching the mighty atom sail through the air can be quite an adventure in itself."

"I am NOT that small." I was indignant. "And if you're going to show him, do it properly, please. You've catapulted me right over the top more than once, if I recall!"

"So I have," he chuckled, but to my relief he gave me a perfect, professional leg up, talking Jason through it as he did so.

I'd made "reins" with the lead rope, attaching it to both sides of Sable's head collar, and I sat on his nicely rounded, comfortable back, feeling quite cocky and sure of myself. Jason limped beside us, moving very fast as he always did.

He looked up at me. "You're a terrific rider,

aren't you. Is it easy to do that?"

"Dead easy," I boasted. "Sandra's not keen on us riding them barebacked and she'd go mad if she saw the horse didn't have a bridle, but I know old Sable so well – "

Old Sable, eager to get back to his field, broke suddenly into trot and I bounced inelegantly, getting left behind. I pulled back on the lead rope, trying to slow him but the naughty cob ignored me and cantered merrily down the sandy lane to his paddock. I was doing fine, slightly breathless with all the pulling, but staying put OK, but I was totally unprepared for the sudden stop Sable put in BEFORE he reached his gate. The horse told me graphically what he thought of me by dropping his head quickly so that I slid ungracefully over his shoulder and down his neck. I lay on the grass, looking up at him and called him a very rude name.

"Kate!" Jason's voice was quite shocked. "What a thing to say! Are you all right? Are you hurt?"

"Just a large dent in my pride." I picked myself up and led the now docile looking Sable into his field. "It serves me right for showing off, doesn't it?"

His face had been dark with concern but a sudden grin lightened it. "You did look funny."

"Har har," I said, somewhat sourly, and latched the gate securely. "Jason, whatever you do, don't tell Sandra, she's – "

"She's at the end of the lane – look," he pointed.

I could see Sandra beckoning and waving. "D'you think she saw – " I began, then started running as I realised what she was calling.

"What's the matter?" Jason, having limped at top speed down the lane to make sure I was all right, was now trying to keep up with me as I charged back towards Sandra.

"Didn't you hear what she said?" I turned my head, hoping my face hadn't gone all white and ghastly. "She's had a phone call from someone whose horse was stolen yesterday. He's coming here to identify Runaway. He'll take his horse away, of course. Oh Jason, I'm never going to see Runaway again. Never."

CHAPTER SEVEN

"H E SOUNDED a really nice man." Sandra was trying to cheer me up. "I mean REALLY nice, Kate. He hasn't slept a wink, he told me, since he discovered his horse had been stolen. He's twenty miles or so away – all country roads – but he's driving here straight away."

"And he's sure Runaway's description matches?" I asked dismally. "What did he say about the snip on his nose? Crescent shaped?"

She hesitated. "He didn't actually mention it. I got the impression the poor man's so demented at losing his horse he just wanted to leap in his car and get to him."

"He'd better remember to bring the horse's papers and stuff," Natalie said darkly. "We won't just hand Runaway over. Anyone could turn up and claim they'd lost their horse."

"But the police phoned him with my number," Sandra said. "This man, Andrew Bartlett his name is, reported the theft of his bay gelding, and then our police told his police about Runaway and his police told him. See?"

"Clear as mud," Jason said cheerfully. "Anyway you can always test him. See if he's aware how Runaway avoids being tied up. If he knows the horse can untie knots then he really does know the horse."

"But the thieves will have worked that out too won't they?" Natalie argued. "Runaway ran away from them by doing that, remember?"

"They'll probably imagine they didn't tie him correctly," Sandra said. "It's a point, Jason, but I'm sure this Andrew Bartlett isn't one of the thieves. He sounded so – so – "

"NICE!" Jason, Nat and I all joined in with her. She nearly blushed. "Well, he did!"

It was only half an hour or so later that Andrew Bartlett arrived at Falconhurst and we could all see she was right. He WAS nice, and even though my heart was sinking at the thought of saying goodbye to Runaway, I was glad he belonged to someone like Andrew. He and Sandra were another pair who seemed to hit it off straight away. Andrew was quite tall and ordinary looking, and pretty old – nearly forty I should think – but he had a kind face and eyes you knew usually twinkled. They were just worried looking when he got out of his car and greeted us, though.

"Would you like some tea or coffee after your drive?" Sandra was smiling rather shyly at him.

He smiled back, the eyes crinkling in an agreeable way. "Mind if I check your horse first? I can't wait to see if it's Oberon."

"Oberon!" I thought in horror. I was about to protest it didn't suit the good-looking Runaway at all, but everyone trooped off to the yard, so I shut up and followed.

Monkey was holding the bay horse, stroking his neck and crooning soothing phrases. Runaway turned his head as soon as he saw us and gave his by now familiar whicker of greeting.

"Does that mean he recognises you?" Jason asked Andrew, looking at him curiously.

The man shook his head ruefully "I wish it did. He's a real beauty but he's not my Obi. I was hoping against hope – " He trailed off and patted the horse, trying to hide his obvious distress.

"I'm so sorry." I felt terribly mean I'd been wishing no one would come and claim the bay horse. "It must be horrible having your horse stolen like this."

"It is, it really is!" The hand that was stroking Runaway's shoulder was trembling a little.

"I wish there was something we could do," Sandra said helplessly. "I was quite sure our bay horse was your bay horse, I hadn't thought any further. Didn't the police give you a full description of the gelding we had here, Mr Bartlett? The snip – "

"Please call me Andrew." He pulled himself together with an effort. "They did, but I thought, I hoped, the mark had been exaggerated. Oberon's very similar in colour and build, a little darker and heavier maybe. He doesn't actually have a snip, but there's an old scar on his nose where the hair grows white. It's only small and not truly crescent shaped but I hoped, I prayed – "

Natalie, although probably affected by his distress as much as anyone, was as cheerfully practical as ever. "In which case we've got a double mystery to solve instead of a single. We just have to track down Runaway's owner AND Andrew's horse. It'll be fun."

"Fun!" Sandra stared at her daughter in disbelief. "You amaze me sometimes, Nat. Where's the fun in traipsing round every market and auction in the country? We've no idea where the thieves were heading. They could have taken Andrew's horse anywhere."

Natalie looked crestfallen but rallied immediately. "We know where they pinched the horsebox from and we know where they dumped it. Two big fat clues for a start. And Jason actually saw them. Clue number three!"

"I couldn't give a proper description of them, I told you." Poor Jason looked embarrassed again, but she waved that aside.

"You'll probably recognise the skinny one when you see him again. Then Andrew can pounce on him and do a citizens' arrest."

Both Andrew and Jason grinned reluctantly.

"Just like that, you see." Sandra smiled at them. "Come on over and have this coffee now. I'll phone the police and tell them I've still got the lost, stolen or strayed bay horse."

"You can ask them if they've got any leads on the case." Natalie was brimming with enthusiasm for her detecting idea.

"I'll put Runaway back in the field, shall I?" I took the horse from Monkey and started to walk out of the yard.

Jason immediately left the others and followed me, though I noticed his limp was more pronounced than before.

"You don't have to come with me if your leg's hurting," I said, and watched his face darken briefly.

"It's OK, I want to." He sat on the gate watching Runaway and me have a little goodbye chat and cuddle, and when I joined him he'd lost the angry, shuttered look and was smiling at us.

"That's better." I pretended to clip his ear. "You look a lot nicer when you're not sulking."

He grabbed a handful of my hair in retaliation. "I do not sulk. I'm just not used to discussing my leg."

"I don't suppose you are if you put on a face like a grizzly bear every time it's mentioned." I disentangled my curls. "You'll have to discuss it with Sandra when you start your riding lessons."

"We're going to an equestrian centre run by the RDA tomorrow." He looked excited and worried at the same time. "Sandra's wanted to watch them at work for ages, she said, so we hope we'll both gain from it."

"RDA? Oh the Riding for the Disabled Association. She wants to do some specialist training with them, doesn't she?"

"Yes." He put out a hand to stop me getting off the gate. "Can we sit here just a bit longer? My leg IS aching a bit. When I saw you fall off Sable I tried to run to you and I've never been able to do that. I just hope it doesn't mean I'm not going to be able to ride."

I was really touched he'd been so concerned at my sudden departure from the wicked old Sable.

"That's obviously one of the things Sandra will be checking out tomorrow," I said, trying to keep my voice cheerful and positive. "And if there's no danger of you making your leg worse by riding she'll have you jumping cavaletti in no time, you'll see."

"What are cav – oh look at Runaway, he's having a funny five minutes."

The bay horse had enjoyed another good roll and was now galloping exuberantly round the paddock, putting in the odd high-flying buck for good measure.

"He's probably bored." I watched his wonderful, fluid action in admiration. "On a normal day he'd be working, jumping, maybe competing. He'll soon get fed up, stuck in a field all day."

"Oh well." Jason climbed stiffly down from the gate. "It's a shame he and Andrew don't belong together but I suppose it's only a matter of time before his owner does turn up."

But that was where he was wrong. Day after day passed and no one came to claim the bay horse. Sandra had several phone calls from people who'd had horses stolen, but not one of their animals had the distinctive white snip.

"Some of the callers have been in floods of tears." Sandra looked really upset when she told us. "One has been looking for her bay pony for months. She's had him twelve years, he's only 14 hh, nothing like Runaway at all, but she phoned us because she tries every lead she ever hears.

"Andrew does too, doesn't he?" Natalie said. "You saw him again last night and he told you he's still searching for Oberon."

"Mm." Sandra looked quite pretty when she blushed. "He – Andrew – took me out to dinner. He said whenever he gets the chance he stops at riding schools, hunter yards, even at fields by the roadside and just checks to see if his Obi is there."

"That's just what I'd be like if my horse was taken." I stroked one of the cats sleeping in my lap. "That's why I can't understand why Runaway's real owner hasn't phoned. The horse is such a darling – "

"Yeah, yeah, we know. We've heard you a hundred times." Natalie threw a cushion at me and both cats leapt off, all eight sets of claws jabbing my legs.

"Ow!" I flung the cushion back, hard. "You're just as boring about Rio. And I bet Runaway could knock spots off her, so I'm right to rave about him."

"It's all very well raving." Sandra looked irritated. "But what good is he stuck in MY field eating all MY grub? If he's going to be here much longer he's going to have to start earning a living. I think I'll ride him tomorrow and see what he's capable of."

"He's wonderful," I said eagerly. "Really well schooled, properly balanced and forward going. I'm sure he'll jump – "

"Oh really?" Sandra raised her eyebrows. "And you get all this information just by looking at him, do you Kate?"

It was my turn to blush. I hung my red face and muttered something about "ust trying him before he went".

"You horror. I thought you were the sensible, cautious one." Sandra wasn't too mad, much to my relief. "As you're so sure of him and so keen, you can get on and do some work with him then. There's the Shepwick Show in a couple of weeks and if Runaway's still here, still eating me out of house and home, you can enter him and contribute some prize money towards his keep."

I nearly fainted. I felt light headed and woozy, just like I did when Jason smiled at me. I rushed to tell him when he arrived the next morning. He came to Falconhurst every day, learning both riding and stable management with an enthusiasm and skill it was amazing to see. After the first couple of lessons, when it became clear he was not only able to ride but had a real talent and aptitude for it, Sandra had been to see his parents. They were reluctant at first, his mother particularly being terrified he'd make the leg worse, or fall and injure himself, but between them, Jason and Sandra wore both his mum and dad down. They'd agreed to pay for a full course of riding lessons and Jason negotiated to finance the stable ones by working through Falconhurst's never ending chores with Monkey, Sandra, Nat and me.

It was a brilliant arrangement from everyone's point of view. Especially mine because we saw each other every day! Now I'd be riding the wonderful Runaway too and I thought I'd burst with happiness. Natalie, in her usual generous way, was thrilled to bits for me.

She and Jason still didn't get on too well. He thought she was loud and pushy and she said he was too deep and moody, but they both liked me so they put up with each other, which was flattering. From now on I'd be putting in a lot more schooling and jumping with Runaway, which would make the slightly lazy Nat do the same on Rio. We all decided to put in some solid riding work for the next two weeks and see what happened at the Shepwick Show.

"I'll even give my detective work a rest," Natalie announced. "Mum's still in touch with Andrew and we've been writing letters and ringing people when we hear horse thieves have been operating. Andrew's taken photos of Oberon and Runaway round to all the local horsey places. No one's come forward to say they know them so I'm running out of ideas. Maybe after the show –"

"Maybe after the show Runaway's owner will be found." I thought and pushed the dreaded idea away.

For two weeks, unless that owner appeared unexpectedly, I could pretend the bay horse was mine and ride him every day. And for two glorious weeks that's just what I did.

CHAPTER EIGHT

SANDRA WAS PLEASED with the way we'd worked. "It's done you the world of good having some decent competition to jump against," she told Natalie. "You've had to try much harder now Kate's a real contender. As for you, Tiger Kate, I didn't think you had it in you. You and the Runaway bay are quite a partnership."

My smile was so big it took up most of my face. I'd secretly feared I "didn't have it in me" either and that I wouldn't be able to do justice to Runaway's obvious talents. He was very fast and very bold and he jumped like a stag – and he went better for me than anyone else, even Sandra herself. He didn't have the streak of sheer brilliance that Rio sometimes amazed us with but he more than made up for that by being totally honest and genuine. I fell off a few times nevertheless. You always do when you do a lot of jumping but it was always me doing something wrong, not him. Nat would crease up laughing at the expression on the bay horse's face when he stood waiting for me to climb back aboard.

"He always looks as though he can't understand what you're playing at, leaving him suddenly like that," she hooted, hanging on to her dizzily dancing mare on the last practice day.

"I expect he does," I sighed and brushed myself down. "My fault yet again. He took the corner perfectly, I just lost it at that last fence. Sorry, Runaway. What a dope I am."

"I think you're doing great." Jason was doing ring steward duties, raising poles and re-assembling fences. "I'm still trying to master changing diaganals at the trot."

I heaved myself back in the saddle and grinned at him. "Don't be so modest. You're coming on really well. Sandra said so."

"Kate! Jason!" Natalie yelled impatiently. "Stop making eyes and whispering sweet nothings to each other. We've got to get it perfect today. The show's tomorrow."

As if I needed reminding. I was already dry mouthed and sticky palmed at the thought and when the alarm clock shrilled at six the next morning I felt as though I hadn't slept a wink. We rolled into our old clothes and did the stable chores before starting on the washing, shampooing, plaiting and polishing needed to make the two horses look their very best. Jason came whizzing in on his bike, nice and early and incredibly helpful. When every hair and hoof was shining to our satisfaction Sandra called us into the house and bullied Natalie and me into eating some breakfast.

Jason, who wasn't competing, happily munched his way through acres of toast and cereal while we pushed some cornflakes round a bowl and felt sick. Sandra, who was also in a couple of classes but is much more used to it than us, was very calm and cheerful at first, but that changed when the post arrived.

"Can you believe that!" She slapped a letter on the kitchen table so hard it made the cups rattle. "Those awful, AWFUL people!"

Jason stared at her open mouthed. Nat and I knew who she meant straight away.

"Not the Grays again!" Natalie groaned and picked the letter up. "What are they moaning about this time?"

"Dung," Sandra said succinctly. "They are writing to me, and to the council, mind you, to complain that my horses drop dung on the road."

"What do they expect them to drop – flower petals? Honestly, Mum, you're going to have to sort that miserable couple out."

"I can't." Sandra ran a hand wildly through her previously tidy hair. "They won't listen to reason. They just don't want us here and they've got worse since the Runaway night. They've complained about the noise from the yard in the morning, our horsebox coming in, our horsebox going out, clients' cars parked outside, children chattering while they ride, even the sound of the horses hooves on the road. They've written reams saying how much they hate the sight, the sound and the smell of us and the poor old council have to investigate every time. It's driving me mad."

"If they dislike Falconhurst so much, why don't they move?" Jason was bewildered.

"They think WE should be the ones to go and I'm starting to agree. I really am beginning to lose heart. There isn't masses of open country to ride in so I need to expand the teaching facilities. If I could only afford to build an indoor school I could take on the work I'd really love to do with the RDA. As it is I think I'll pack it in and go and run a sweet shop."

"Don't you dare!" Jason was clearing the table with his usual efficiency. "I need you, remember. You can't give up on me now I'm just getting the hang of things."

"Or me." I gave poor Sandra a quick hug, she looked so fed up. "Come on, put it out of your mind and go and enjoy the show. We're all going to be winners, you'll see."

She was still subdued and unhappy when we arrived at the showground, but then we saw Andrew walking towards us and we knew she'd be all right.

"I didn't know you were going to be here today." She really did look quite pretty when she blushed, I thought.

"You don't mind do you? I'd like to cheer you all on and I've brought my camera to record the prize giving. I'm glad to see you're all looking very smart. Most important when you go up to receive your cup."

"Whew, nothing like being overconfident!" Sandra laughed with him, the worried frown leaving her face at last. "Though we've threatened Kate if she doesn't win, she and that stray horse of hers will be thrown out on the streets."

"Quite right. About time they earned a living." Andrew winked at us and Natalie and I climbed aboard our shining steeds and started walking them round to warm up.

"What time's your first class?" Jason looked up at me and patted my leg comfortingly.

"It's the next one. We'll try the practice jump in a minute."

"I'll go and set it up." He limped rapidly away and I followed, trying to fight down the panic attack my nerves were threatening me with.

Once Runaway was warmed up I tried out the single pole Jason had set up. It was fairly low and quite simple but I lost contact, misjudged the ground line completely and my poor horse had to bucket over it as best he could.

Even Jason pulled a face and I could hear Natalie's sarky intake of breath from right across the ground. I cantered Runaway in a twenty metre circle, took some deep breaths myself, and tried again. This time we flew it and as my confidence grew so my nerves receded.

Jason obligingly changed the height and shape of the jump a few times and I felt at least halfway ready to meet the real thing. I reported in at my class and asked Jason to keep Runaway on the move while Natalie walked the course with me.

"Lead him round, you mean?" he said.

"No, you can ride him while I sit on Ranting Rio and walk a bit of sense into her," Sandra told him. "Don't look so worried, we're not asking you to jump these fences – that's Tiger Kate's job."

Jason swung easily into the bay horse's saddle and followed Rio's shining chestnut rump.

As they left us I heard him say, "Runaway's great but rather Kate than me. Those jumps look enormous."

They looked even bigger from where I was standing. I gulped several times and tried to listen to what Natalie was saying about the number of strides between fences three and four and the need to approach number seven at a slight angle.

"Are you taking this in?" she demanded. "You're looking positively glassy eyed. What's the matter?"

"I've never – " My voice came out in a squeak and I tried again. "I've only done a few jumping classes and they were very junior stuff. I can't believe I'll get round this lot."

"There's nothing here you and Runaway

haven't tackled." Nat ran a professional eye over the whole course. "Apart from a formal water jump, but you've cleared the stream on the common with him haven't you? So – no problem, all you have to do is concentrate."

"That's all right then," I tried to be flippant. "Nothing to it really."

She grinned and took me to every jump, talking me through each turn and takeoff, each approach and landing.

"Aren't you nervous?" I demanded, watching her examine the solid looking wall.

"Terrified!" She grinned all the same. "I know Rio can do it of course, she's actually done bigger classes than this, but she's so erratic. She just might decide to take fright at the flower urn and throw me straight through these blocks, or pretend she's scared of that 'Road Closed' sign and stop dead. At least with Runaway you know he'll try."

"Oh I know it's not the horse who's the problem, it's the rider." I was fighting to stop my teeth chattering with fear. "Maybe you should take him round, Nat. You're not scared of anything."

"Wanna bet?" She held out her hand which was shaking like a leaf. "I'm petrified too and going round with Rio's plenty for me, thanks. Anyway, the stray boy doesn't go well for me. He'll do anything for you so just give it a crack."

Sandra said the same thing when they came

back with the horses.

"Just do your best and ENJOY it." She gave me a leg up into the saddle. "I'm only kidding about you winning. I'll be really proud of all four of you if you get round."

Natalie was first to go. She looked as cool as a cucumber as she rode into the ring. She did a few dressage steps to calm the excited Rio, then the chestnut mare was cantering through the start and approaching the first fence. I watched every move, wincing as Rio fought for her head coming into the big double and admiring the way Natalie held her together, timing each part of the jump perfectly. The water was no problem at all, the mare cleared it with masses to spare, and they were cantering the last turn and coming towards the red wall. For one horrible moment I thought Nat had been right about the flower displays at each side. Rio seemed to roll her eyes briefly at them but a light touch on her flanks reminded her of the job in hand and she was soaring, flying high to land perfectly.

"A clear round. Clear for Miss Natalie Clements and Lady Rio de Janeiro," crackled the loud-speaker. "Next to go is Number Forty Eight, Mr David Davidson riding Vikings Valentino."

We watched Valentino crash his way through the first three jumps, refuse once at the water and knock the complete top layer off the wall.

"Nineteen faults," the loudspeaker said.

"Nineteen for Mr David Davidson and Vikings Valentino. Next to go is Miss Kate Harvey riding Runaway Bay."

I don't remember leaving the collecting ring, or asking for canter, but the video film Andrew took shows Runaway and me smoothly approaching the start, looking totally poised and confident. Luckily the camera was too far away for the microphone to pick up the sound of my knees knocking. The first jump, a simple one of rustic poles, was upon us before I'd settled. I misjudged it and took off too far back, but Runaway stretched to his utmost and just rattled it slightly as he came down. Amazingly that brought me to my senses, and I got the next approach and takeoff dead right, turning in the air to meet number three, a fearsome looking spread.

I thought we'd touched a pole but nothing fell and we were still cantering, controlled and buoyant, towards the next line of fences. The sensation of power and speed was exhilarating and to my surprise I realised I actually WAS enjoying myself. I wondered for an instant about the water, but Runaway was having a good time too, and didn't give it a second glance. We got the angle dead right for number seven's approach and before I knew it the last jump, the hefty looking wall, was coming up and we were still going perfectly.

I sensed a slight hesitation in the bay horse's approach and I picked him up and urged him on, driving him forward with my legs and seat. He took heart immediately and soared over the red blocks, clearing them by a mile, to land beautifully and canter on through the finish. As applause broke out from the crowd he did a happy little buck, throwing up his heels and making the people laugh and clap even louder.

"A clear round. Lovely clear from Kate Harvey and Runaway Bay. Next to go – "

I didn't hear any more. I rode from the ring with the sound of the crowd in my ears, a big silly grin on my face, and the most wonderful horse in the world as my partner. My friends gathered round to pat and thump and yell their congratulations and I sat there, smiling and quite incapable of dismounting. Jason put a hand up to help me and I slid down, almost into his arms.

"None of that, you two!" Nat was almost dancing with delight. "Oh well DONE, Kate you devil. We're both in the jump-off!"

The jump-off. I'd forgotten about that. "You mean I have to do it AGAIN!"

Everyone laughed, and Jason and I put Runaway's sweat rug on and walked him round to cool down while watching the rest of the class. There were over twenty entries and only four in the jump-off so we'd already done brilliantly.

"I don't fancy my chances against the clock though," I confided to Jason. "Nat and Rio are like quicksilver. If they go clear there's no way I can catch them."

"Just do what Sandra said." Jason looked reassuringly proud of me. "Enjoy it and do your best. No one expected you to get this far."

He was right but my heart sank for an instant when I saw the way Natalie and Rio flew the jump-off course. They didn't put a foot wrong and knocked three whole seconds off the early leader. Runaway and I went well, though we didn't have the speed when turning, but to my delight we were still quicker than the other horse, putting us into second behind Nat and Rio.

"Wonderful! wonderful!" Sandra was hopping up and down. "Don't be disappointed you two girls if the last to go pips you at the post. This girl rides all over the country and her horse is a real speed merchant."

The grey gelding could certainly shift and we all watched as they screamed round the course, cutting vital corners and clearing everything in their path. They were going nearly flat out when they galloped at the wall and the grey got in a bit too close, shifting the top brick as he went up. The crowd gasped as he came into land then groaned in sympathy when the block came with him – four faults and fourth place.

Natalie and I went to collect the cup and red rosette for her, blue (plus MONEY) for me, Andrew's film showing me going through the whole ceremony still wearing that same dopey grin. When I saw it the next day I told Natalie I'd need drama lessons to learn not to do that, but she said a nice big paper bag over my head would do just as well. Charming girl. I was busily bashing her with a cushion when Sandra came into the room. She switched the TV off and stepped over us almost absent mindedly.

"Gerroff, Kate!" Nat pushed me away and sat up. "What are you thinking about Mum? You look miles away."

"Andrew's just been telling me about the show next week at the Diamond Centre." Her face was pink and excited. "It's a bit of a high flyer for us – we've never entered anything as big, but you both did so well at Shepwick he thinks I ought to put you in for it."

"All in favour shout AYE," Natalie yelled immediately "AYE. Come on Kate, you're in favour. Riding Runaway at a place like the Diamond! It'll be like a dream come true. Rio's bound to win of course, she's so brilliant – "

Her mother picked up the cushion and socked her with it. "I can see why you do this," she said to me. "I didn't hear you say AYE, little Kate. Don't you like the idea?"

"It's a bit frightening," I admitted. "I'm relatively new to all this, you know."

"You are indeed. And I certainly won't push you. You ride our mystery horse so well it seems a shame not to take the chance while you've got it though."

"It's funny but I've started thinking of Runaway as Kate's horse now, haven't you?" Natalie said casually.

I flinched and Sandra patted my shoulder understandingly. "Unfortunately that's one thing we mustn't do. Someone, somewhere owns that lovely horse and presumably one day they're going to come forward. You do know that, don't you Kate? He can't really be a horse from Nowhere."

"Yes I do know," I said, trying not to go all weepy. "And you're right, it would be silly not to enter him in the Diamond Show while I can. Who knows – someone there might recognise our Runaway and solve the mystery."

"Course!" Natalie stared at me. "It's where the thieves stole the horsebox from isn't it? Clue number one I called it and I've never followed it up."

"So you're definitely going in for the show?" Sandra looked at me carefully.

I nodded. "Yup. And I think we might even beat Nat and Rio this time."

"Good for you, Kate. Now you're sure you're all right?"

"Sure." I tidied the cushions, bending my head so they wouldn't see the tears in my eyes.

Tears that were never far away at the mention of losing my wonderful, wonderful Runaway.

CHAPTER NINE

Luckily from then on we were so busy working I didn't have time to dwell on the awful thought. Apart from our normal riding school chores we had just the week to practise, practise, practise. The more I rode Runaway the better we "gelled"' and the more my confidence grew. He was as sweet as ever too, seeming to enjoy all the activity as well as the good food and company he was getting.

Before we knew it, show time was upon us again. Diamond Day, Jason called it, and he was as excited as Nat and me. There were just the two horses going this time, Rio and Runaway, so we were taking the trailer not the horsebox. Monkey and the freelance BHSI were running Falconhurst for the day and Sandra and Jason would be coming in the Land Rover with us.

"A groom each, there's luxury!" Natalie pretended to polish her nails. "We can just swan about looking wonderfully professional, Kate, while these two do all the work."

"Dream on," her mother said succinctly. "Andrew's meeting us at the Diamond. He wants to put in some serious detective work looking for Oberon, so I'll be busy helping him."

"Oh surprise, surprise!" Natalie said cheekily.

"And I dare say Kate and Jason will be tracking down Runaway's owners in dark little corners. Looks like I'm the gooseberry again."

"Don't be daft." Her teasing about Jason still embarrassed me. "I'll be involved with the jumping won't I? I won't get much chance to do any detecting."

"Not that you're terribly keen anyway. Andrew's absolutely desperate to find out where his horse has gone but you'd rather go on as you are with Runaway wouldn't you?" She can be very cutting at times.

"Give it a rest Motor Mouth." Jason was really annoyed with her. "Kate's got enough to worry about today. Anyway she's already asked me to do some snooping around on the Runaway trail for her."

That wasn't strictly true but it was nice of him to stand up for me.

We left Falconhurst quite early – it was a three hour drive to the Diamond Centre – and as we drove carefully along the lane we saw Mr and Mrs Gray tidying their already tidy garden. As soon as they heard the Land Rover and the slight rattle of the trailer they looked up sharply and Mrs Gray actually shook her fist.

"Oh no, there goes another letter of complaint." Sandra sighed and clouted the steering wheel in irritation. "She'll have a note to the council in by first post telling them how I drive noisy horse transporters past their house at unsociable hours."

"But you're not waking them or anything," Jason said. "They're already up and about, so how can they moan?"

"I don't know but they will." Poor Sandra looked dejected and Natalie started muttering about "rotten old fogies who know nothing about horses" etc. etc...

Jason and I looked at each other and wondered how to cheer them up. Three hours is a long time to be cooped up in a car with two grumpy people.

Once we'd left the Grays a few miles behind, however, they both seemed to shake off the miseries and we sang and played silly childish car games, until suddenly we were driving down a wide, tree-lined avenue, and there, against a smartly painted post and rail fence, was the familiar dark red diamond sign.

"We're here!" I yelled. "Oh WOW!"

Not very eloquent but it seemed to sum the place up. The Diamond Centre was simply fabulous. Lush paddocks, huge indoor manege, an incredible cross-country course swooping through beautifully wooded grounds, the most perfect stabling you've ever seen – and of course the horses. To reach the show-jumping arena we had to drive through security gates, where our competitor passes were carefully checked, then negotiate an immaculate curving drive through the stud farm. The grounds stretched way back to secluded pastures and stabling but even in the nearby paddocks there were mares with their foals, beautiful, highly bred and totally delightful. We all oohed and aahed at them as we followed the long driveway, slowly rounding each paddock with its sophisticated security gate and observation cameras.

"Coo, Kate, you're going to be a film star again." Nat wiggled her fingers at a nearby camera and I pretended to fluff out my hair and do an actress pout.

"Very pretty," Sandra said drily. "Come back to earth little Tiger, your class is in less than an hour!"

At least I didn't have time to tremble. We had loads to do, warming up to get on with, schedules to check – and a course to walk. I did it all as in a dream. Natalie was only second to go in our class and she and Rio went clear.

"They really are working brilliantly," I said to Sandra and she looked incredibly proud.

"It's because they've been putting in so much work, there's no substitute. And it's made all the difference having you and Runaway to sharpen them up." She patted my shoulder. "You can do it too, you know, don't you doubt it."

I more than doubted it, having walked the superhuman course, but to my amazement, we hardly put a foot wrong and were the seventh clear round.

"It's going to be one heck of a jump-off." Nat was chewing her lip. "They're all real quality horses and so fast! I thought Rio could fly but – "

"She can and I think you two are unbeatable," I said loyally.

Jason scowled and muttered something about me being too modest but I thought he was just being kind. No one else managed a clear so it was the seven of us into the final jump-off, a shortened course against the clock. Natalie was first to go and everyone could see she meant business. She and her incredible crazy, talented horse swooped round the ring like a gleaming fiery arrow. Everyone gasped at the lightning speed of their turns and their bold perfection of jumping. Natalie herself was thrilled with her beloved mare's performance.

"I told you she was going to be special." She was laughing delightedly and hugging her mother.

Sandra, beaming with joy and pride, hugged her back and said, "It took a lot of work to bring it out and you've done it! Brilliant, darling, absolutely brilliant!"

I sat on Runaway in the collecting ring, feeling oddly detached as if all this was happening to someone else and I wouldn't really have to follow that. Nat came over with me and we watched the next four go round, all slower and one with four faults. The next to go was a sleek, black horse ridden by a long-legged girl in smart black boots and jacket.

"These two are terrific," Natalie breathed. "If anyone can beat our time they can".

The athletic looking horse and rider took the first three jumps as fast as Nat and Rio had, but their turn into number four looked fractionally slower.

"If they're going to win they'll have to spin between the gate and the big oxer," Nat said. "I went round the gate because I thought it was too tight, but I think you and Runaway should try it. This girl is – look."

The black horse wheeled sharply at the girl's command but couldn't straighten up in time for the final jump. His rider tried to pick him up and he leapt heroically, but with his stride all wrong he clouted the pole hard on his way up. The crowd groaned as it fell and gasped in amazement as his time was announced – faster than Rio – but with four faults.

And now it was my turn. My head felt like cotton wool and my legs had turned to jelly but Runaway moved off when I asked him as if he noticed nothing amiss. Jason was by the ringside, dark face intent, brown eyes full of pride and encouragement.

"Go for it!" he yelled. "I know you can do it, Kate."

My head cleared and my strength returned. "We made it here," I told the beautiful bay horse. "So let's give it our best shot."

I felt part of him, moulded into his being, we were moving and working as one. We took the first four jumps splendidly, perfectly attuned and as fast as Natalie and Rio. But not faster. Our only chance was in the final turn as Nat had said – spin between the gate and the oxer, two long strides a "bounce", jump the big upright and Bob's-your-uncle. I'd never asked for such a turn, never felt sure enough of myself to try anything that bold, but today on Runaway I felt I could take on the world. The brave horse took the turn, pivoting sharply and barely cutting his speed. The angle looked impossible from here but he lengthened his stride and one – two – three, we were soaring cleanly, wonderfully over the coloured poles, to land, pick up and gallop for the finish. Even before the crowd burst into spontaneous excited cheers, before the loudspeaker made its crackling exultant announcement, I knew we'd won. I patted and hugged and shouted and Runaway joined in the celebrations by kicking up his heels in his joyous "winning buck".

The crowd laughed and cheered again and I felt

two big, salty tears running down my face. I rode out of the ring and slid down Runaway's back into Jason's strong, warm arms. His good-looking face was pressed close to mine and I thought I was going to burst with pride and happiness. He drew back at last and gently wiped the tears away. Natalie, Sandra and Andrew came running over and I realised just what I'd done.

"Oh Nat, Natalie I'm so sor– " I began but she thumped me, excitedly hugging and laughing.

"Don't you dare say sorry! You were wonderful, that was so, so brave."

"We're very, very proud of you." Sandra hugged me too and even Andrew gave me a cuddle.

People all around were looking and smiling, enjoying our happiness. I felt incredibly joyful and lucky to have such wonderful, unselfish friends and loved collecting our prizes and cantering the lap of honour. I was busily untacking Runaway, giving him whole packets of polos, when Andrew came over again, this time looking solemn.

"You really did do well," he began hesitantly. "And I didn't say anything before the jump-off because Sandra and Nat didn't want anything to put you off."

"Put me – " I stared at him. "What – oh Andrew, you've found something out about Runaway!"

"I told you I was going to do some more what your friend calls detecting while we were here" He shuffled his feet.

"I was showing the photos around, you know the ones I carry of Oberon and Runaway. Once again no one recognised Obi, but a girl, one of the in-hand judges actually, thought she knew Runaway."

"Where – is she still here?" My throat had gone dry.

"Yes, she works here, schools the young horses being brought on by the Diamond Centre. Her name's Karen, she came across to watch you in the first round of your class and says she definitely knows the horse."

"Is he hers – why didn't she get in touch – can I speak to her – ?" I felt confused and stunned, the elated feeling gone, leaving a dull, heavy something in the pit of my stomach.

"She's just finishing up in ring three, then she'll be over – ah – Karen."

The girl was smart and efficient looking, in her early twenties with that indefinable air of horsey superiority. She was nice though.

"Hello Kate. I've just heard you won your class. Well done indeed!"

"Thank you – er – Karen. Andrew says you recognised Runaway." I closed my eyes for an instant. "Come and have a closer look."

I turned the bay horse to face her and she ran a hand lightly over the snip on his nose. "This is the real giveaway isn't it? But I'd have known him anyway once I saw you riding him. I always thought he had a wonderful action and you've certainly brought out the best in him."

"Wh – what's his real name?" I asked faintly.

"There's a mystery here then? Andrew gave me a rough outline of how he ended up with you so I'll fill in what gaps I can."

"Thank you." I was being very polite, very controlled.

"His name is Saracen Prince – Saracen because of the snip – you know, crescent shaped like their curved swords – and he was born and bred here at the Diamond. I brought him on, schooled him and we did fairly well in a few BSJA shows – though not as well as you!"

"So is he still yours?" I was heartbroken, truly heartbroken. Nice girl, wonderful premises and I knew I couldn't bear to leave him here. "The police said the Diamond Centre told them only a horsebox was stolen."

"That's true," she shrugged. "We're absolutely paranoid about our horses, no one can get in or out of a paddock or stable, but the lorry park's proved to be not as secure. Saracen Prince was no longer here TO be stolen though – he was sold a few months ago."

"So why didn't his new owners report it?" I was fighting hard not to cry.

"I honestly don't know." She looked sympathetic if a bit embarrassed at all this emotion.

"Karen's going to find out the name of the people who bought Run – Saracen Prince," Andrew put in.

"I'll do my best." The girl gave the bay horse a last pat and turned away. "I don't have anything to do with the selling side but I'll go over to our office and ask them to check their records."

"It's very kind of you," I said dully, and Natalie put her arm round me.

"We have to find out don't we?" she said. "It would be dreadful if someone took him away in months to come when you were really fond of him."

I wanted to scream that it was too late, I was already really, REALLY fond of the horse but I knew that was unfair and silly. I gulped a lot and got myself under control again. Jason, dark eyes full of concern, came over and suggested a walk.

"I'd like to see some of the other classes," he said diffidently. "Come with me and explain it all, Kate?"

"OK," I tried a slightly wavering grin. "I'll bring Runaway with us so he can cool down." I wasn't going to call him Saracen anything.

I had to walk quite quickly to keep up with Jason's rapid limp. He was very entertaining about the events in some of the other rings and I held tight to the bay horse's lead rope and started to feel better. We were on the edge of the showground now, and Runaway had cooled nicely, his sweat drying rapidly in the warm breeze. I let him drop his head to have a good munch of the Diamond's lush grass, wondering if he remembered it and trying not to think what would happen to us now.

Jason perched on a fence, looking round at everything with interest. Suddenly he stiffened and I saw him crane his neck towards the other side of the fence.

"What is it?" I asked, looking up at him.

"There's someone hanging round the trailers and horseboxes over there." He was screwing his eyes up to see more clearly. "I don't know but – yes – Kate it's that guy! The skinny bloke, the one in the cap – the – "

"Horse thief!" I yelled and Runaway threw up his head in fright.

"I've got to get him." To my horror Jason slipped off the fence the other side and started racing away. "Go and get help Kate," he called back quietly. "I'll try and keep him here. Get Andrew."

I tore across to the fence. "Jason don't be a fool! You can't tackle him alone. Come back and we'll both get Andrew."

He was already approaching the line of horseboxes and I saw him increase his pace, limping swiftly towards the back of a lorry that, surely, had started its engine.

"Stop!" I yelled "We're too late – he's driving away."

The horsebox pulled out and began slowly trundling across the field. Jason followed, easily keeping apace as it bucketed across the ground, then to my utter disbelief he stretched out a strong arm and hauled himself onto the back of the box, clinging on as it picked up speed and headed towards the exit.

CHAPTER TEN

I YELLED "STOP THIEF," and "Jason let GO!" and other idiotic phrases. There was no one to hear me and I spun round frantically looking for help. I could see the horsebox travelling the long, winding drive that led to the Diamond Centre's security gates. Surely the thief would be stopped there, Jason would call out and alert the guards – but what if they couldn't stop the lorry and it got away?

"Once it gets out on the road the thief will race away at top speed. Jason won't be able to hang on. He could be hurt or even killed – " Without thinking any further I looped Runaway's lead rope into reins, clambered on the fence and slid onto his back.

I could still see the roof of the horsebox, being driven slowly and carefully so as not to attract attention. The route looped round Diamond's fields and paddocks and I could see a way I just might be able to stop it. If Runaway and I took a direct line, straight across two fields and the road, we might make it to the gate before the lorry did.

I'd never ridden the bay horse barebacked before and I certainly hadn't attempted anything on him without a bridle. I didn't have any choice. There was just this one chance and I had to risk it.

116

Runaway cantered smoothly off at my command and if he was surprised he didn't show it. We covered the ground swiftly and the solid looking fence surrounding the first paddock was in sight before I knew it. I gritted my teeth and encouraged him onward with everything I'd got.

Without the contact and control of the bit he could easily have refused to jump, ducking out at the last minute, but Runaway's trust in me and his natural courage took us soaring over it. The field was empty, it had been rolled and harrowed and the surface was perfect for our flat-out gallop. The warm wind was in my face and the sheer strength and power of the bay horse beneath me. I'd never, ever been so fast with such little control in my life but I didn't feel afraid. I could only think of Jason, clinging bravely to the back of the horsebox and the need to reach the gate before the thief did.

The fence at the other side of the field was coming up fast and I pushed with my legs, seat, in fact my whole body, to get the same breathtaking leap from my brave horse. We landed safely on the soft turf, took two galloping strides to cross the drive, straight into another take-off to jump the thick hedge bordering the second field. I could see the horsebox out of the corner of my eye. It had passed the spot we'd just crossed and was on its way to the gate. I kept my body forward and streamlined and Runaway kept going, as straight and fast as a bullet.

Although the lorry was ahead of us its route was longer. If we could maintain this pace we could just do it. Another hedge, thick and fairly high. There must be a gate somewhere, I thought, but it wasn't in our line of vision and there was certainly no chance of stopping to look for it. We were approaching the hedge, going fast and I could actually see the security guards standing by the gate.

They spotted us too, and if I hadn't been so intent on the job in hand, I'd have laughed at the incredulous expressions on their faces. I gave the merest of touches this time and felt Runaway's muscles tense and bunch in preparation. We flew over the solid hedging without so much as a scratch from a twig and my only problem was how to stop. Remembering the futile yanking on Sable's headcollar I tried simply sitting back and saying in a calm, decisive way, "Whoa Runaway. And – halt."

The nearest guard was showing the whites of his eyes as we thundered towards him and he gave a look of sheer relief when we slowed almost immediately and stopped, only centimetres from him.

I slid off and yelled "Shut the gates! Please, you've got to shut the gates!"

Whether it was the passion in my voice or the

dramatic way we'd arrived, they asked no questions and to my great joy the big electronic gates slid smoothly into place just as the horsebox turned the last corner on its approach to the exit. The driver saw them closing and reacted instantly, slamming on the brakes and wrenching open the cab door.

"Stop that man!" I was screeching again. "He's stealing that lorry and he steals horses too!"

The poor security guards, who'd been having a nice quiet day till I arrived, were slower to move. The horsethief jumped down from the driver's seat and doubled back, racing away from the gates and heading for the perimeter fence.

"He's going to get away," I moaned, then caught my breath as a tall figure threw himself across the grass verge in a brilliant rugby tackle, bringing the man crashing to the ground.

"Jason!" I turned to the still stunned guards. "Quick, help him. He's caught the thief!"

"Where the 'eck did the lad come from?" They ran over to Jason and the driver who were struggling and fighting on the grass, and hauled the horsethief to his feet, pinning his arms safely behind him.

Jason was panting and dishevelled, and blood was trickling from a cut on his lip, but he grinned in delight when he saw me.

"Are you OK?" I wanted to run to him but I was

still holding Runaway and anyway the security men were looking.

"Bit of a bumpy ride but I managed to hold on. Thank god they closed the gates before we got onto the road. I take it you got them to do that. How on earth did you get here before us?"

"I hacked over," I said lightly, and hugged Runaway hard.

"They came flying over the hedge at us like a bloomin' guided missile," one of the guards said and Jason laughed.

"Tiger Kate in action!"

"After all that I just hope you can verify your story about this driver," the other guard said severely.

"Just ask him what he was doing with this lorry." Jason looked at the cringing thief. "I don't think he'll be able to explain why he fiddled with the wiring on the ignition so he wouldn't need a key."

"And I bet he doesn't even know the name on the horsebox side." I glared at the nasty looking individual. "Don't look round, just tell us what it says."

He tried glaring back but he could only bluster and whine.

"Clear enough." The security men marched him firmly back to their gateside office. "We'll alert the horsebox's owner over the show's tannoy. The police are going to be pleased to make Matey-Boy's acquaintance. This is the second lorry stolen from our premises – he's getting too cheeky by half. They'll need your evidence of course – you'd better leave your names and addresses."

We gave them all our details and gladly left the snivelling thief with them.

"Maybe you'd better ride ahead so you can let Andrew know about this straight away." Jason smiled at me but I could see he was hurting. "I can't move too fast so – "

"You do the riding then." I gave him a leg up before he could argue. "Is that more comfortable?"

"Mm. Runaway won't gallop off and jump fences with me will he?"

"Not unless you ask him to." I gave a quick hug to the bay's strong neck. "We've had enough excitement for one day I should think, so let's just plod quietly back to the showground and find the others. Andrew will want to see that ghastly man before the police take him away won't he?"

"That's just what I thought," Jason agreed. "He'll want to know exactly where he took Oberon after he stole him."

"I just hope he decides to make a full confession," I said. "Apparently they get lighter sentences if they admit to everything and show some sign of remorse."

"Remorse! Andrew will knock his block off if he

doesn't tell him about Obi." Jason chuckled at the thought.

"You had a good go at that yourself." I pretended to sound severe. "Clinging on the back of a moving lorry then wrestling a horsethief to the ground! Not what your mother had in mind when she agreed to you learning how to ride."

He smiled and moved his leg a little stiffly. "Well maybe I won't do that particular exercise every day – but the rest of my new life is great." He paused and looked at me, quite shyly. "Really, really great."

I blushed and pretended to brush something off Runaway's shoulder, feeling warm yet trembly at the look in Jason's dark eyes.

It took a lot longer to get back to Diamond's showground now we were taking the conventional route. Natalie, Sandra and Andrew were sitting drinking coffee and watching a showing class, quite unperturbed at our absence.

"What have you two been up to?" Nat glanced at us casually. "You look as if you've been pulled through a hedge backwards, Jason."

"He's just been hanging by his fingertips on the back of a stolen lorry and launching himself through the air to bring a horsethief crashing down," I said nonchalantly. "Nothing much!"

"And Kate's been galloping across country, leaping six-foot hedges and controlling Runaway with nothing more than a bit of string." Jason was exaggerating of course, but I rather liked it.

"What!" Sandra squealed and turned to look at us properly. "What's this about, Kate? You say Jason caught the thief?"

"Not just me. Between us," Jason said modestly. "It was mostly Kate and Runaway. They're the real heroes."

"What – how – ?" All three of them started together.

We managed to calm them down and tell the story. They were very flattering about what we'd done and Andrew, as we'd thought, couldn't wait to do his own bit of "interviewing" to find out where Oberon had been taken.

"And Runaway?" Sandra looked at me gently. "Where did this man steal him from? Did you get the address?"

I flushed a very deep red. "I didn't – I don't – " I broke off, not wanting to admit it hadn't crossed my mind to ask the weasely horsethief just where the bay horse he'd lost in Wheelers Lane had come from originally.

"Don't worry Kate," Sandra said kindly. "You did wonderfully well ,the pair of you. With all that excitement it's no wonder you forgot to ask."

I saw Natalie give me a knowing look. She realised that deep down I didn't WANT to find Runaway's owners and that was probably the reason it hadn't occurred to me to do any "detecting".

"Andrew will probably get all the information from the police when they've taken the horsethief's statement," Sandra was continuing. "And anyway, Karen, the girl who works here, has gone off to look the Diamond Centre's records up. That will show us who bought Saracen Prince and the address he was sent to."

"Oh good," I said dismally and she patted my back in sympathy.

"I know it's tough but we really do have to find out don't we?"

"I don't see why," I burst out. "They obviously don't love him the way I do and we're looking after him really well aren't we? Even Karen said he'd never looked better and he won the jumping class and – "

"That's another thing," she looked worried. "I wasn't going to say anything today but Karen thinks we shouldn't be competing with Sar – Runaway. She says legally we should only be exercising him to keep him reasonably fit, nothing else. I told her we didn't use him in the riding school, but she says we should find out from the RSPCA how we stand in law."

"That's silly," I said flatly. "What about the money it's costing you to keep him – food and blacksmith and all that?"

"She says I can bill the owner when we find him. Oh please don't cry, Kate, we warned you not to get too fond of this horse."

I couldn't help crying. It seemed so unfair when Runaway and I had worked so hard and done so well. I stuffed the lead rope in Jason's hand and, blinded by tears of sadness and anger, ran as far away as I could from the beautiful, wonderful horse who belonged to someone else.

CHAPTER ELEVEN

MY LITTLE TEMPER TANTRUM didn't last long. I had a good weep, then wandered back to Falconhurst's trailer and did some tidying up. Jason saw me and came over with a huge chocolate icecream. There's something very cheering up about slurping an icecream, and I didn't want to wreck the day for everyone else so I stopped sulking. Natalie had entered another class with Rio and, with the chestnut mare in such brilliant form, won it easily. I wondered sadly if I'd ever, ever experience the heady sensation of winning again, but was wholeheartedly thrilled for Nat when she went up to collect her prize.

Andrew came back from his visit to the police with an address to check out for Oberon. He was so thrilled, so absolutely overjoyed at the prospect of finding his beloved horse that you couldn't help feeling happy for him. He asked Sandra to go with him the following day, and they discussed strategy, their heads close together.

"He's holding her hand," Natalie announced in a stage whisper. "Isn't it lovely?"

Jason looked at her. "Are you taking the mickey as usual or do you mean that?"

"I mean it," she was indignant. "I really like Andrew and Mum could do with a bit of romance.

She's not all that old."

It still seemed odd to think of the two adults in that light, but as Jason said, Andrew had been divorced for four years and Nat's father died when she was only eight, so it was about time they'd thawed out.

"You make them sound like a couple of frozen haddock," Natalie grumbled, throwing some grass at him. "You're about as romantic as – I was going to say cold rice pud but I LIKE cold rice pud!"

She stalked off and Jason said very quietly to me, "And I like YOU my tiger Kate."

We touched hands briefly and I knew from the look in his eyes he felt the same glorious tingle I did. Unlike Natalie I found him a great deal more romantic than any kind of pud!

The journey back to Falconhurst was quieter than our outward trip. Sandra hummed softly, obviously deep in happy Andrew thought, but Natalie was asleep before we reached the end of Diamond's drive. Jason and I sat together, talking quietly till I felt my eyes grow heavy and I nodded off too, my head resting nicely on his shoulder.

The next day felt uncomfortably flat, not just with the usual anticlimax after a show. I woke with the awful heaviness that a deep sadness brings, the dreadful ache in the pit of your stomach when you know something horrible is about to happen, the feeling I was beginning to think of as

"Runaway Misery". My parents had been thrilled to pieces with the cup I'd brought home from the Diamond and couldn't understand why I seemed so down in the dumps.

"I had no idea you were so good at showjumping." My mum kissed me in amazement. "You should have said it was such a big do and we'd have come up to watch you. I hope that's not why you're so blue today."

"No, of course not. It was miles away and I thought you'd be bored," I said. "No one was more surprised than me to win."

"Next time we'll definitely come." Mum was still looking anxious. "Won't we dear?"

"Yes, of course we will." My dad was looking bemused too. "Well done Kate!"

"There won't be a next time." I fought back the tears. "I'll never get the chance to ride Runaway again. I told you about him not being claimed didn't I? Well, Sandra's got the address of the owners now. We're going down there to see them the day after tomorrow."

"From what you've told us they're not much cop as owners," Mum said loyally. "Maybe they don't want him back, Kate. They'll probably be glad someone like you has got him."

"I don't think so." I tried to smile, they were both being so understanding. "He's worth a lot of money – I don't know why they haven't come forward so far but once they know where he is they'll want him back if only to sell him again."

"Can't we buy him then?" Dad nearly took my breath away.

My parents are lovely but so un-animally we don't even own a hamster.

I hugged him. "I wish we could but as I say he'll be expensive. Far too expensive for us."

"Are you sure?" he asked anxiously. "We've been thinking of buying you a horse for a long time and this seems to be the one you love most."

"Oh I do!" I burst into tears. "And if we could only afford him I'd be the happiest – "

"Look," Dad said. "I'll tell you what I could pay and we'll take it from there."

I told Sandra and she gave me one of her brief, fierce hugs. "Saracen Prince is worth double that I'm afraid. Don't cry though, Kate, if there's any way of working something out we'll do it. We're all on your side you know."

I did know and I was grateful to my friends and family but I didn't hold out much hope. Money talks as they say and Runaway's price tag was shouting far too loud.

"It's no good walking around with a face like a sick sheep," Natalie said in that loving way of hers. "Mum and Andrew are Oberon hunting today so you've got Runaway for another twenty-four hours at least. Make the most of it."

She was right of course but I was finding it really hard to raise my spirits knowing the brave and beautiful horse would soon be gone. I felt apathetic and listless and I couldn't bear to even look at Runaway in case I started crying again. Jason was busy in the yard but I noticed he kept glancing worriedly at me from under his eyelashes.

"I don't suppose you'd do something for me?" he said diffidently as I wandered aimlessly past.

"Sure," I said. "What would you like?"

"Sandra says I can start hacking out, nothing too fiery, just a little amble across the common. I wondered if you and Runaway would come with me?"

I felt my smile freeze. I'd already decided not to ride the bay horse again, to try and cut myself off from him completely. "I thought he should have the day off," I lied. "I'll take Amber out with you if you like though."

Natalie came out of Rio's stable and stared at me. "Mum said Runaway should be given an hour or so of quiet riding," she said, "So he doesn't stiffen up after yesterday's shenanigans. I've got to wait for the blacksmith for Rio, she's cast a shoe, but you and Jason could go out now. It would be ideal."

I pretended I didn't know the bay horse should be taken out but I wasn't fooling either Nat or

Jason. I tried to be cheerful, and chatted away while we tacked up Limerick, the big Irish mare Jason was going to ride. I even managed a smile as we left the yard and walked sedately along the lane, but when we reached the little patch of common my self-control took a nose dive and I had to turn away so Jason wouldn't see the tears trickling down my face.

"Come on Kate," he said gently. "If you're not going to see Runaway again you've got to say goodbye haven't you? And if things work out and you are – well enjoy today anyway, it's the only thing to do."

He, like everybody else, was being so kind, I cried even harder. Limerick, feeling the turf under her feet, was beginning to fidget and Jason looked a little worried when she started to dance.

"She doesn't do this in the school Kate," he said, "What do I do?"

"Relax." I sniffed unbeautifully, but stopped crying. "You've stiffened up, that'll make her worse. I'll lead on shall I, and Limerick will soon settle down again."

The common was ablaze with golden spikes of broom and gorse and purple heather bloomed alongside the sandy tracks. Runaway went beautifully as usual, ears pricked forward and intelligent eyes looking at everything with interest. I kept an eye on Jason, who was doing really well on the big mare. We went into a warming trot, had a nice little canter, and I found I was enjoying myself again.

"That's better." Jason's grin was cheekier than ever. "You needed that. You look less like death warmed up now."

"I thought we came out because YOU needed the ride." I looked at him suspiciously and his grin grew even wider.

"Not me. I wasn't going to try this till I'd had another couple of lessons in the school but I'll do anything for a good cause."

"Oh yeah, I come into that category do I?" I pretended to glare. "I've a good mind to make you gallop home."

"Don't do it!" He begged, still laughing. "Runaway should be kept nice and quiet remember, and my leg's still giving me aggravation from yesterday."

"Oh Jason, I'm sorry." I felt immediately contrite. "I wasn't thinking. I'm so wrapped up worrying about this horse."

"It's OK, Tiger Kate. I've really enjoyed my first proper outing. Let's hope it's the start of many."

I firmly pushed away the thought that it was probably the very last for me on Runaway. If Jason could risk his first ride in the great outdoors just to cheer me up today, the least I could do was BE cheered up. We walked coolingly back to

Falconhurst. It was late afternoon and to our excitement we saw Andrew's big car and trailer in the distance, heading for home too.

"Can you see if he's got Obi?" Jason shouted.

"No, they're too far away," I called over my shoulder. "They're turning into the drive now. Wow, I hope it's good news."

When we rode into the yard a few minutes later we could see it was. Andrew was standing there, wreathed in smiles, proudly holding a lead rope attached to a very ordinary, slightly scruffy bay horse. Jason and I put the horses in their stables and rushed over.

"Here he is!" If Andrew's grin got any broader it would be round the back of his head as well. "He's lost weight and he's very dirty but isn't he GREAT!"

"Great," we both echoed politely and patted the horse kindly. He blew down his nose in friendly fashion and took a handful of pony nuts hungrily but very gently.

"He'll soon get his condition back." Sandra was running her hand expertly down the horse's legs. "And they haven't spoilt his manners, that's one good thing."

"Why is he here?" Natalie joined in the welcome tickle and scratch routine Oberon was enjoying.

"I wanted your mum to have a good look at him here in the daylight," Andrew said, "and the rest of you of course. I knew you'd want to be part of the celebration. I still can't believe I've got him back."

"He looks really pleased to see you too," I said, watching Obi rubbing his head up and down Andrew's shoulder. "Where did you find him? Did you have to buy him back?"

"We'll just sort him out," Sandra said, "then we'll be over to the house to tell you all about it. Put some plates to warm, Andrew's bought us all a Chinese takeaway."

"Ooh yum." Nat was off and running towards the kitchen.

Jason and I finished doing Limerick and Runaway, then put them back out in their paddock.

"Funny," Jason said as we walked back to the house. "I pictured Oberon quite differently. A sort of cross between Runaway and Champion the Wonder Horse from what Andrew said."

"That's obviously how a doting owner sees him," I laughed. "Obi looks very nice, at least he will when he's cleaned and fattened up a bit, but as you say he's just average in our eyes. I'm so glad for Andrew though, he deserves to get him back. Have you ever seen a bigger smile?"

The smile was still there all the way through the delicious Chinese meal. It only disapppeared when he described the awful, run-down old farm he and Sandra had visited earlier.

"We had a real job to find it," he explained. "Your horsethief did a lot of singing yesterday, including the main address where he offloads batches of stolen horses. The poor animals are shoved in a scrubby field for a while until a suitable horse sale comes up, more or less anywhere in the country. That way the trail's confused and any leads are cold. These louts forge receipts and sell the horses to anyone who wants them."

"So they aren't selected for any particular reason," I asked. "I thought perhaps the thieves went for quality – like Runaway."

"No. From what I could see they tend to be nondescript, no striking colours or distinctive marks. They'd probably have dyed Runaway's snip if they'd managed to keep hold of him. They'd disguised a couple of blazes and the odd star quite successfully the police told me."

"So how did you find this place in the end?" Jason said. "Did you go in with the police?"

"I wanted to," Sandra said. "But Andrew wouldn't wait. He was afraid to waste any more time and give them a chance to get rid of Obi if they hadn't already. We drove round and round looking for this farm. There wasn't even a nearby village where we could ask, but we found a track in the end."

"I drove along it as far as I could," Andrew went on. "It led to this decrepit old house and yard, but I didn't take the car in there."

"We hid it in a wood." Sandra was looking at Andrew almost besottedly. "I was quite scared but Andrew was like – like – "

"Like a Tiger Kate?" Natalie put in helpfully and we all laughed.

"Yes, just like that. We slid through the wood on foot and picked up the track again, where it snaked past the old house."

"It was miles from nowhere." They were like a double act, taking it in turns. "Muddy, neglected old lane, bounded by rickety fencing. There were no hoofprints, no sounds, no anything much at all. But I had a feeling, a really strong feeling that this was it."

"I wanted to go back to the car," Sandra admitted. "There were no signs of horses anywhere but Andrew wouldn't give up. He stood on a tree stump, put two fingers in his mouth and let out the most piercing whistle."

"I've done it ever since I had Obi," Andrew explained proudly. "I keep him at the place I work, it's a sheep farm as you know, and it's huge. I can't walk all over it when I want my horse so I taught him to come to me."

"Wow!" Jason, Natalie and I were deeply impressed.

136

"So did Oberon suddenly appear over the hill, thundering towards you like in a Black Beauty film?" Natalie asked breathlessly.

"Not quite." His smile was back now. "But I listened, listened very carefully and I heard him."

"I did too," Sandra said. "Quite faint, but it was enough to take us in the right direction. We followed the sound across two potato fields and through another scrubby copse."

"I realised we were doubling back, working our way behind the old farmhouse we'd seen." Andrew was really enjoying himself. "We pushed through the brambles in the wood and as the ground cleared we could see into a rough little field that had six or seven horses in it. And waiting for us, looking straight at us over the fence, was –

"Oberon!" we all yelled.

"I was thrilled of course," Sandra joined in, "but scared of what Andrew would do next. We couldn't get Obi out the way we'd come of course, so the only route was straight up through the farm yard."

"S'truth!" Jason was staring in awe. "What did you do – take the whole gang on single handed – sorry Sandra I didn't mean to exclude you."

"Perfectly all right," she said cheerfully. "I've already said I was frightened to death of any confrontation but as it happened we got the timing absolutely spot on. Just as Andrew was making a fuss of Obi a whole group of people appeared at the gate."

"The horsethief gang!" Natalie gasped. "Was there a fight? This is better than a book."

Andrew shot her an amused glance. "Sorry to disappoint you but the people consisted of a middle-aged couple and four policemen. The couple lived in the house and were busily denying to the visiting police that the horses in the field were stolen. They said they were all 'pets'."

"I can just imagine their faces when they saw you in the field with their so-called pets," I chuckled. "How did they explain you to the police?"

"How could they?" He laughed and hugged Sandra. "We left them watching out of their window as we loaded Obi into the trailer. The owners of the other horses will be contacted of course, but the officer in charge was quite happy to let me take Obi away from the ghastly place luckily. They've got a clear-cut case thanks to your thief capture yesterday. He's named everyone involved in the ring and they'll all be rounded up."

"Wonderful," Natalie sighed. "I just wish I'd been involved a bit more. I was quite keen to do some detecting and solve our two mysteries but you seem to have managed without me."

"Never mind." Andrew patted her lightly.

"We're only halfway through remember. I'm all right thank goodness but there's still the poor devil who owns Runaway to sort out. Maybe you can do that, Natalie."

She looked at me uneasily. "No I don't think so. It's not the same thing at all."

"She's right there," I thought, my fists clenching. "Finding Oberon is a dream come true but our other mystery's the exact opposite – just one big nightmare."

CHAPTER TWELVE

I HAD ONE MORE NIGHT before it began in earnest. I was staying at Falconhurst again. Sandra had decided we should definitely visit the address of the people who'd bought Saracen Prince from The Diamond.

"It's another early start," she said, "So get a good night's sleep you two. I've phoned the number Karen wrote down at least a dozen times, but I just get no reply. Andrew and I did so well turning up in person for Oberon, I've got the feeling it's the only way. If no one's home we can ask around, find out from neighbours or other horse owners just what's going on."

We agreed and I felt that at least if I was DOING SOMETHING I'd feel better. I'd been happily hiding my head in the sand, hoping no one was going to turn up, but now we'd discovered some of Runaway's past it made the ownership question more "real life" and I could no longer go on pretending he was a horse from nowhere. The ride out on the common with Jason had done me good, stopping me sinking into depression and making me at least face up to the future. I was confused though. I thought it was great, the lengths Jason had gone to to make me happy, so I was taken aback when he said he wouldn't be coming on the following day's "detection" trip. It was the Falconhurst horses day off, the day in the week when there were no lessons, no riding, so he could easily have joined us. I wasn't going to beg him or anything, if he didn't want to be with me then that was that, but I was secretly pretty upset.

I was also feeling sentimental about Runaway, and for two pins I'd have gladly slept in the stable, watching over the bay horse for our one last night. My down-to-earth friend wasn't having any of that though.

"Runaway's perfectly happy turned out in the paddock with Limerick," she said. "It's a lovely fine night and he doesn't want to be stuck inside just so you can do your watchdog act. You're going over the top again Kate, you should cool down. You don't see me getting myself in a knot like this."

"It's easy for you," I grumbled unfairly. "Here's me, for the first time ever with the chance to buy my own horse and the only one in the world I want is out of the question. I could be calm if I had nothing to worry about like you."

"Nothing to – " She picked up a pillow and hurled it at my head. "What about the trouble the Grays are making for Falconhurst? My mum's at the end of her tether with them and she can't take much more. If it wasn't for Andrew – and that's another thing." She sounded so impassioned and unlike her usual laid-back self I was startled out of my own self pity.

"What is it Nat?" I'd been poised to fling the pillow back but I put it down. "I thought you liked Andrew."

"I do." She threw herself on the bed. "I think he's great, ideal for Mum and they really like each other. But now he's got Oberon back he won't have any excuse to come and see her will he?"

"Why should he need an excuse?" I asked in surprise.

"Honestly Kate, I sometimes think you go around with your eyes shut. Because he's shy that's why. It was easier for him to meet us at shows and to take Mum out to tell her about his 'detecting'."

"I've never thought of him as shy," I said defensively, picturing Andrew's unassuming manner. "But now you've said it I can see just what you mean. But your mum isn't shy. If Sandra wants to see him she will."

"Oh yeah, she'll go chasing after him just the way you do with Jason."

"I certainly do NOT – " I began in a rage and she pounded the bed with her fists and feet.

"I KNOW you don't Kate, that's my point. Even though you like him you wait for him to do the running. It's difficult when you like someone and you know they like you too, but you don't want to make a fool of yourself in case you're more serious about it than they are."

It wasn't very grammatically phrased, but it summed up very well the muddly way I was feeling right then.

"And it's like that for Sandra and Andrew?" I was amazed, I always thought they were such confident people.

"Yes, I think it is. And if they don't see each other any more now the Oberon mystery is solved, they'll drift apart before they ever really get together. Then who knows what will happen to Falconhurst?"

I frowned, she'd lost me there. "How do the Grays and Falconhurst fit in with all this?"

"They don't as such, except that I can see Mum giving in to their complaining and deciding to stop running the riding school. She's been on her own for years and no one works harder but she's tired. Tired of fighting on her own, and, without Andrew, I think she'd be ready to pack it in."

"Oh Nat, what will happen to the horses – Rio and Amber, Sable and the others?"

She hid her face. "I don't know. Without the school we couldn't afford to keep them could we?"

I felt terrible. There I was, spending half my time fretting over Runaway and the other half doubting whether Jason liked me enough to stay around, when all along my best friend was worrying herself sick over far heavier problems. I walked over and touched her awkwardly on the shoulder. Her face was still buried in the duvet and her fine blonde hair was tumbled and messy.

"Natalie I'm sorry. I've been so absorbed with Runaway and Jason – I didn't know you were so unhappy."

She sat up and rubbed her face dry. "Oh I'm not. I'm mostly OK and I've been really glad for you getting on so well with the horse and with Jason too. I'm probably just feeling left out."

"You're certainly not left out." I picked up a strand of her hair. "You're still number one with your mum, you know that, and you'll always be my best mate. And to prove it I'll do you a Kate Harvey Special Hairdo. You'll look so great some passing millionaire will spot you tomorrow and leave you all his money. Then you can buy the Diamond Centre and stick your tongue out at the Grays."

"I do that anyway," she said with a shadow of her usual grin. "Every time I pass their bungalow."

"Come on then." I thought it was best to change the subject, "Wash and Brushup time!"

We spent the rest of the evening doing our hair and trying out makeup and nail varnish and when I finally went to sleep I found my dreams weren't sad and emotional as I'd dreaded, but full of hope. Sandra noticed the change first thing the next day.

"Hello," she smiled at me. "Do I see the light of battle back in your eyes Kate?"

"Yup," I said. "I've decided to be very firm with these people if we find them today. I'll let them explain why they didn't make any effort to track Runaway down and if it's not a good enough reason I'll insist they sell him to me. At my price of course."

She roared with laughter. "Really? What's got into you? You've been all tears and defeatism since Karen identified Saracen Prince."

"Runaway," I corrected her. "He'll always be Runaway to me."

"What did you say to this girl last night Natalie?" her mother demanded, still laughing.

Nat smiled, her shining hair surrounding her face like an angel's wings. "I just mentioned not giving up or giving in. I don't believe anyone should do that do you?" she said innocently, the old teasing light back in her eyes.

"I think you're deeper than you let on." Sandra gave her an affectionate hug. "But however you did it I'm glad you got Kate motivated anyway."

"One down – one to go." Nat was back on form with a vengeance and I nudged her so she wouldn't take it too far.

The three of us were making the forty-or-so-mile trip in the Land Rover.

"I don't suppose Andrew will turn up at this

place today will he?" Natalie said it oh so casually.

"I shouldn't think so." Sandra's face was carefully noncommital. "Now he's got his adored horse back there's no reason for him to carry on detecting is there?"

"Will you give him a ring when we get back to let him know how we got on?" Nat persisted.

"No, I'll wait till he calls here. He said he'd let me know how Oberon goes on, so I'll leave it till then."

I saw exactly what my friend had meant and I pondered about the complexity of people's emotions. Sandra was acting exactly the same way about Andrew as I was with Jason, both of us needing similar reassurance it seemed.

We drove on, going very carefully past the Grays' house.

"Don't want to give them another reason to moan," Sandra was almost whispering. "I really couldn't take another letter from the council."

I saw Natalie's fingers clench and she turned away from her mother and made a hideous face at the prim bungalow. Very childish I thought – and made an even worse one. We were all rather determinedly cheerful on the journey. Natalie and Sandra were doing their best to keep my spirits up and now I realised what a strain they were both under I felt obliged not to worry them by being miserable.

"I just hope this isn't going to turn out to be a complete waste of time." Sandra was driving on the inside lane of the motorway. "If they're away on holiday or something we could find ourselves just turning round and coming straight back."

"You said we could ask around locally though didn't you?" I said. "Check with neighbours if they remembered seeing Runaway there and so on."

"Yes. We really must get to the bottom of this. I had no idea we shouldn't have been using Saracen – sorry Kate – Runaway – the way we did. What worries me is if the Grays find out. They know the horse we found isn't ours and if they snoop around in their usual charming way someone might tell them Kate's ridden him in a couple of shows. If that's against the law as Karen said they're bound to cause trouble over it."

"Ye gods," Nat exploded. "Everything we do is spoilt by that horrible couple. You're scared to breathe half the time aren't you, Mum?"

Sandra glanced quickly at her.

"I'm not getting at you," Natalie said wearily. "I just wish we could get them off our backs and out of our lives."

"Not much chance of that," her mother said sadly. "Get the map out and look for this village will you, Nat?"

We found the address Karen had given us quite

quickly. It was a newish, very smart detached house on the outskirts of the village. There were vertical blinds at all the windows so you couldn't see in, and a glossy front door with a brass lion's head.

Sandra rapped the lion smartly several times. The door stayed firmly shut and no one peeked between the blinds.

"Shall I try next door?" Natalie started walking to the next house.

There were only a few houses along the road, all set in their own grounds of an acre or so. We could see the one next door had a swimming pool and some artistic landscaping. Runaway's address was harder to peer into, being heavily screened by trees and fencing at the back. Sandra and I could hear dogs barking at Natalie's approach and saw the front door open. It was too far away to be able to hear what she said but it was obvious a fairly animated conversation was going on.

"Nat's finding out the neighbour's life story from the look of it." Sandra was grinning.

"I hope they're not telling her anything bad about Runaway." I felt horribly tense and nervous now we were here. "Maybe these people were cruel to him and a horse rescue organisation had to be called in."

"Kate!" Sandra said in exasperation. "You're letting your imagination run riot again. Runaway was perfectly fit and well when we found him – upset at his experience but certainly showing no signs of being ill treated. We're going to find out what happened so stop thinking up horror stories."

"Sorry." I peered across to the still chatting Natalie. "Whatever are those two saying?"

"Maybe I should go over – no, here she comes."

Natalie ran back to us, calling a polite goodbye over her shoulder.

"What did she say? Was Runaway here? Did they know he'd been stolen?" The questions were tumbling from my mouth.

"Hang on Tiger. Stop yer growling." Natalie shook back her hair and took a deep breath. "She said an awful lot actually, considering the first thing she told me was that the people in this house keep very much to themselves and don't have much to do with any of the neighbours. Apparently Runaway arrived here a few months back. The neighbour says she remembers a cream lorry with a red diamond on it bringing him here."

"That fits," I breathed.

"Quite. She, the neighbour, says she was surprised to see the horse because she got the impression they, the Albanys they're called, weren't that keen to have a horse."

"If the Albanys don't talk to her much how did she reach that conclusion?" Sandra was still trying to peer through the fencing at the back of the house.

"Mrs Nosey Neighbour says when they moved in here earlier this year, one of the first things Mr and Mrs Albany did was go across and take a look at her swimming pool. Mrs N N tells me this house has a little stable block and a paddock round the back but the Albanys seemed more interested in having a pool and a pretty garden like hers."

"There's no accounting for taste," I said. "Why did they buy Runaway then? Did Mrs Nosey know?"

"She hated to admit it but she didn't. She says the horse arrived, she saw the Albany's daughter, Helen, ride it a few times, then a few weeks ago another kind of horsebox turned up, Runaway was loaded into it and that's the last she saw of him. Since then Helen has disappeared completely and her parents are hardly ever here. They run a business somewhere she thinks but she doesn't know what it is."

"It must be torment for her living next to such a mysterious family." I couldn't help grinning at the thought. "She's the sort who wants a chatty coffee morning at least once a week so she can keep up with all the gossip."

"I wish we knew where the Albanys work." Sandra was looking worried. "From the sound of it they resold Runaway very rapidly and we need to find out who bought him."

"Why would they buy a horse just to sell him again?" I was perplexed. "Especially one like Runaway. He's so lovely – "

"Don't let her start on that," Natalie told her mother, "She'll never stop. Could the Albanys be dealers do you think?"

"Horse dealers don't generally live in this type of area," Sandra said drily. "The setup's all wrong. We have to find out where Runaway went from here. Any ideas?"

We looked at each other blankly.

"Where's the paper where Karen wrote this address?" I asked. "I don't suppose she put the Albanys' business one on the back did she?"

Sandra looked at it. "No, just this one – oh that's funny."

"What is?" Nat crowded up to look.

"The address is this one but Karen's put the name down as Banfold. W Banfold, it's quite clear."

"Perhaps someone else lives here who's called that," Nat said. "Shall I go back and ask the neighbour?"

"No we mustn't trouble her again." Sandra frowned. "I know. Let's find a phone box and see if there's a Banfold listed in the local book."

We bundled back into the Land Rover and turned it round to drive back the way we'd come.

We all saw the pretty drapes move at the house next door and knew the helpful Mrs Nosey Neighbour was watching us. There was a phone booth about half a mile down the road. I hopped out and brought the directory back to the car. Sandra ran her finger down the page.

"Banfold. Banfold. There aren't many and only one W. He's listed as living in the next village – it's just a couple of miles further on. Is he worth a try do you think?"

"Definitely," we said. Even I was determined to get to the bottom of the Runaway mystery by now. We drove on, found the village and after a little argumentative navigation down some twisting, turning lanes, found the house. All three of us did a simultaneous intake of breath. It was beautiful, quite old and built of lovely mellow stone that seemed to grow out of the soil itself. Ivy grew thickly on the walls and around the leaded windows.

It was reached by a curving drive of creamy gravel which we drove along in Sandra's somewhat scruffy old Land Rover, feeling quite overawed.

"Back door or front?" Sandra asked. "Are we visitors do you reckon or will W Banfold think of us as tradesmen?"

"Visitors," I said firmly, "investigative visitors."

"Ooh get you." Natalie had gone quite quiet.

"Look Kate, you can just see a stable yard. It looks beautiful too."

"It also looks deserted." Sandra frowned and tried to tidy her hair with one hand.

We drew up outside the heavy oak door and bunched close together as Natalie pressed the bell. It seemed ages before any one answered. I was imagining a very correct and snooty English butler and Nat was picturing someone in a Count Dracula cape, so it was quite an anticlimax to see a pleasant faced middle-aged woman.

"Mrs Banfold?" Sandra extended her hand politely. "I'm Sandra Clements. I wondered if I might ask you some questions about a horse."

"There is no Mrs Banfold." The woman hesitated. "I'm the housekeeper. I suppose it's Mr Banfold you'll want to see but he won't like talking about horses I'm afraid."

We all thought that was a peculiar thing to say and the housekeeper obviously saw as much in our faces.

She lowered her voice. "He hasn't been able to ride for a number of years you see. There was the business of that horse he bought for his grand-daughter but – "

"Who is it?" We hadn't heard the rubber wheels of the chair and all jumped at the irritable voice from behind her.

"It's a Mrs Clements, sir. About a horse she said

– I was just explaining – "

"We don't need to do any explaining." He was an old man, white haired and frail looking but his voice still had a powerful edge to it. "I suppose the Albanys are trying to sell him to you are they?" He glared at us all. "It's him I blame – Helen and her mother wouldn't act this way. They stole that animal back – it's not theirs to sell d'you hear?" He turned the wheelchair and said to the housekeeper, "Shut the door. That's all I need to say to them."

"Please," Sanda said desperately. "You don't understand. We're trying to find Run – Saracen Prince's owner. The Albanys – "

"The Albanys," he emphasised the name as if he hated it, "are not the horse's owners. I have told you that and it is all I have to tell you."

"But we – ". I tried to say, "we've got him. We've got Saracen Prince", but I found I was saying it to the massive and very firmly shut front door.

"Well," Sandra was shaken to the core. "How incredibly rude!"

"If I was confused before I got here I can't think how to describe what I am now." Natalie shook her head in disbelief and we all walked dazedly back to the car.

CHAPTER THIRTEEN

SANDRA'S DRIVING showed how much the old man's rudeness had upset her – instead of her usual slow and steady pace she took the Land Rover to seventy miles an hour for the whole length of the motorway bit! When we pulled into Falconhurst's drive it was still only late morning and Monkey's wrinkled face showed his surprise.

"With all that detecting you had to do, I didn't think you'd be back till after lunch," he said.

"We didn't hang about," Sandra said shortly, "There was no point. And no, before you ask, we didn't get anything sorted out. I'm beginning to feel I'm totally incapable of dealing with people."

She stomped off in one direction, and, after waiting to see if Jason would appear, I felt the same, and disappeared in another.

I could hear Monkey asking Nat, "What's got into those two? Was it something I said?"

"No," I thought. "It's not you, Monkey, it's Jason. He doesn't care enough to be here."

I went straight to Runaway's paddock. He was on the far side of the field, but as soon as he heard me he cantered straight to me, mane and tail streaming. He was so beautiful, so kind, yet he'd been moved around, pushed from one place to another and still it seemed no one would say where he belonged.

"You belong to me," I whispered in his ear. "In my heart anyway. I'm no nearer owning you legally and I can't see us getting anywhere with that horrible old Banfold. What are we going to do, Runaway?"

"Talk about it to Jason," a deep voice said and I glanced up, startled.

"That was the horse speaking." He grinned in his usual heart-wrenching way but I didn't smile back. "Runaway wants you to tell me all your troubles."

"Does he?" I turned back to the horse. "Doesn't he know you aren't that interested?"

"Kate, Kate." Jason pulled me to him gently. "Are you saying that because I didn't go with you this morning?"

I gulped and tried to pull away. "Yes. No. It doesn't matter."

He wouldn't let me go. "It does matter. I thought, I really thought, you wanted Natalie to help you sort it out. You keep telling me she's your best friend and you don't want to leave her out of things."

"She is and I don't." I sniffed and wouldn't meet his eye. "But that doesn't mean I don't want you there. We needed you today – it was awful, this old man practically threw us out."

He tilted my chin and made me look at him.

"I'm sorry. If you'd asked I'd have been there like a shot. But you didn't ask."

"I thought you'd know I wanted you – " I could feel tears trickling down my face.

Jason wiped them away and hugged me gently to him. "I didn't. I need to be told sometimes, everyone does."

"OK." I made a huge effort and stopped crying. "If I tell you what happened will you help me now?"

"Yes. Fire away."

Runaway stayed near us, cropping the grass contentedly while I went through the strange events of the morning.

"It doesn't make sense." Jason frowned, and scratched his head with the hand that wasn't holding mine. "We've got to get in and talk to this Mr Banfold. Karen gave you his name as being Runaway's owner, and he told you the horse definitely doesn't belong to the Albanys, so it's Banfold who holds the key."

"But it's impossible to go any further with him. We went to his house, it's beautiful by the way, loads of land, he must be incredibly rich. We were perfectly polite and ready to explain the position and he just wouldn't listen. He slammed the door in our faces while we were trying to tell him we've found his horse."

"He does know Runaway's been stolen does he?

What was it he said about that?"

I tried to remember, "He was talking about the Albanys – he had real dislike in his voice – and he said something like 'It's him I blame, he made them steal the animal back.'"

"Steal it back," Jason said thoughtfully. "That certainly doesn't make sense. Back from where? – the Albanys haven't got the horse obviously – so what makes the old man say THEY stole it?"

I saw what he was trying to get at. "He's under the impression Runaway's still with the Albanys isn't he? He said something about them trying to sell the horse to us. He thought that was why we were there." I shivered in remembrance. "His face was all twisted and bitter and yet he sounded almost triumphant when he told us they weren't the owners."

"We've got to talk to him again." Jason was decisive. "There's no other way."

"It's hopeless. He'll probably refuse to see us and anyway I can't see Sandra doing another hour's driving just to have a door shut in her face again."

"She won't need to. We'll go by train. Just the two of us. We can put our bikes in the ' van and cycle from the nearest station." He patted Runaway and started limping back towards the yard.

As he still had a firm grip on my hand, I went

too though we detached hands once we were in sight of the house. Monkey was pottering around in the tack room. Even on days off he likes to work at this and that.

"That's better Mighty Mouse." He pulled a hideous face at me. "You're looking a bit more human than when you arrived. Did Jason kiss it better?"

"Wouldn't tell you if I had." Jason's grin showed how much advance he's made on the teasing front. "Is that Andrew's car I see?"

"Sure is. We're not to tell Sandra, but Natalie phoned him from the office. Told him her mum had been badly upset by this old geezer Banfold. You should have heard Nat, 'I don't want to trouble you but I'm really worried about my mother. What'll I do?' She'd hardly put the phone down and Andrew was pulling in at the drive."

I looked at my watch. "We've only been back forty minutes. He must have dropped everything and just flown here."

"Ain't love grand," Monkey said cryptically, giving Jason a knowing wink.

There was no sign of Andrew or Sandra when we reached the kitchen. Nat was busy making a pile of sandwiches.

"Where's – " I began but she shushed me quickly.

"They're in the living room. I think Mum's

crying on his shoulder. Isn't is great?"

Jason looked perplexed but I knew what she meant. We'd decided not to tell Nat about Jason's train/bike plan. It wasn't meant as a deliberate exclusion, neither of us thought she'd go for the idea anyway. She was so angry at Banfold for distressing her mother she wanted nothing more to do with him. On the way home she'd described him as a dreadful old man and said if the Albanys were even half as bad, not one of them deserved to have Runaway back. Natalie, in fact, was all for me keeping the horse and not taking the ownership mystery any further. Of course Sandra wouldn't hear of it and had pointed out that it would make us no better than horse thieves ourselves. So, Jason and I just helped my friend with the lunchtime sarnies and didn't mention the afternoon's trip at all.

Natalie made us promise not to let on she'd phoned Andrew. "I'll tell Mum later." She was straining her ears to hear the two in the next room. "But I want her to think he rushed over without any prompting. It'll make her feel better."

Sandra certainly looked better when she and Andrew finally came in to join us. Both the colour in her cheeks and the confidence in her manner had returned.

"Andrew's got straight down to his detecting, AND he's got results." She smiled at us. "Isn't it nice that he came over today?"

"Nice," we echoed solemnly.

"What have you found out?" Nat demanded. "We've been all over the place this morning and not unravelled a thing and you haven't been anywhere yet."

"Sleuthing by phone it's called." He winked at her conspiriatorally. "And I will admit I had a big advantage. I actually know the Albanys."

"No!" We were like a Greek chorus.

"Mm. As soon as Sandra said the name and the village it rang a bell. I only know him – Derek Albany – and not as a personal friend but I've bought things from him several times. He's an antique dealer, he has a shop not far from me. He's always lived in the flat above it but last time I saw him he mentioned his wife's father-in-law had bought a house for them in the village you visited today."

"Hang on." Jason's intelligent brow was furrowed. "His wife's father-in-law? That's an odd way of putting it. You mean Derek Albany's father?"

"Very quickly spotted," Andrew said approvingly, "No, nothing so simple. I should have said ex-father-in-law. Derek's wife was a widow – formerly married to Mr W Banfold's son – does it make sense now?"

"Right," I said excitedly as the penny dropped.

"And if he's Helen's grandfather then she must be from the first marriage – she's Helen Banfold."

"Exactly. Derek and his wife haven't been married long. When they met – he's just told me all this on the phone as you've realised – she and Helen were living at old man Banfold's house, Swallow Ridge – you went there."

"It's a fabulous place," Natalie said enviously. "Even though he's such a grouch, Helen's dead lucky to have a millionaire for a granddad."

"Well maybe so, but from what Derek Albany's been telling me, it's not been that much fun lately. Of course it must have been hard for the old man having lost his son – Helen's father was killed in a car crash three years ago. The accident also left Mr Banfold crippled and Helen and her mother, Trish, moved into Swallow Ridge to be with him. That was OK for a couple of years but as soon as Trish showed signs of wanting to leave and start leading her own life, the old man became very difficult."

"Poor old thing." Sandra has an incredibly kind and forgiving nature. "They were all he had. Now they've gone it's no wonder he's so bitter and ill tempered."

"I can see that but I do agree with Albany the old man had no right to try and control his daughter-in-law's life. The real crunch came of course when Trish and Derek got married."

"When was that?" I asked.

"Last year some time. Trish and Helen moved into Derek's flat despite rows and threats from Banfold who tried to keep Helen with him. Derek says Trish tried hard, spoke to the old man almost daily and made sure Helen visited regularly but he still played up. Trish was owed money from the sale of her house but Mr Banfold pretended it was all tied up in investments and wouldn't let her have cash."

"He was probably scared she'd take the money and move as far away as she could," Sandra said.

"It's certainly what I'd do." I looked at Natalie. "Wouldn't you?"

"We-e-e-ll," she thought about it. "I've never had a granddad, especially not a millionaire one."

"If Trish couldn't get her money, how did Derek Albany buy that nice new house you saw this morning then?" Jason ignored Nat. "That was worth quite a bit didn't you say?"

"Ah, now we're coming to it." Andrew looked around at us all. "The house you saw first, the address Karen gave you for Runaway, was bought by Mr Banfold and given to Trish and Helen. They had no say in it, no picking and choosing, he just presented it to them a few months back."

"Wow!" Natalie was impressed.

"Wow indeed, but it's not the way things should be done. Derek, from the sound of it, was pretty put out by then. He said to me he didn't like the house, it was too far from his shop, and what did he want with stables and a paddock anyway?"

"Why did old Mr Banfold buy it then?" I was puzzled.

"Because", Jason said, "it's just down the road from him, so he could still keep an eye on things, still have a say in their lives."

"Right again," Andrew nodded. "And of course the stabling was in preparation for Saracen – sorry Kate – Runaway."

"Now you HAVE lost me," Sandra said. "What was the thinking behind buying a horse?"

"When Helen was little she had a pony at Granddad's – her father was a very good rider apparently and she was encouraged to learn. The thing was she didn't ever really take to it, quite nervous and much more interested in music anyway."

"Strange," I shook my head. "You aren't going to tell us Mr Banfold bought a fabulous horse like Runaway just in the hope Helen would be like her dad?"

"No," Andrew frowned, "I've got all this information from Derek Albany remember and he's as mad as hell at the old man still and pretty biased against him, so maybe Banfold's not as mad as he sounds. I think buying Saracen Prince was one last all-out stab at keeping Helen nearby. She's sixteen now and has chosen to go to a music college in the north. Her grandfather didn't want her to go, insisted her talents lay with riding. By buying her a showjumper he thought he could make her stay. But of course it didn't work."

"Mrs Nosey Neighbour told me Helen had ridden the horse a few times," Natalie said. "Then all of a sudden it was taken away, not in a Diamond Centre lorry this time".

"That's just what happened. Like the house, Saracen – Runaway – was literally presented to them. Helen thought he was lovely apparently, but she's too scared to compete. She looked after him properly, exercised him and so on, but she wouldn't change her mind about going away to college in the autumn. Her grandfather went literally mad when he realised he couldn't make her stay. He ranted and raved and sent a hire box over to take the horse away from Helen."

"Poor, poor Runaway." My eyes were burning with angry tears "Like a tug-of-love child in the middle of a stupid fight. Where did the old man take him this time?"

"To Swallow Ridge. His own house. He was probably still hoping to bribe Helen with the horse. And it's at this point where your mystery part of the story comes in."

"Runaway was stolen from Swallow Ridge by our horse thief, if I can call him that," Jason said. "Is that right?"

"Ah, but there's more to it than that. We couldn't understand could we, right from the start, from the first day you found Runaway – "

"Night," Natalie corrected him. "Torn from our beds we were and all because of those noxious Grays – "

"Sorry Natalie," Andrew carried on quickly. "From the very first night you had him, when Kate felt so strongly that something was wrong, we couldn't fathom out why no one ever reported Runaway as missing".

"Exactly," Sandra said. "There you were, following every lead for your stolen horse, and all Runaway's owner had to do was contact the police and they'd be told where he was."

"Are you saying Mr Banfold was so angry at Helen he couldn't care less that the horse was stolen?" I demanded. "That's unbelievable. And what about Helen? Why didn't she – "

"Whoa, whoa. Steady, Tiger!" Andrew put up his hands in mock fright. "Here's how it happened. Helen contacted her grandfather straight away to make sure Saracen Prince was all right. They had a huge and terrible row and she said she couldn't stand any more. She left to spend the summer in France with friends of Derek and Trish. The next thing Derek knew was a furious phone call from the old man accusing him of trying to steal the horse. They'd tied him up in the old yard one morning – and found him running loose in the kitchen garden an hour later. Banfold said that Albany had obviously sneaked into Swallow Ridge with the intention of stealing the horse back so they could sell him."

"You're kidding," I breathed. "Didn't your friend tell the old man that Runaway can undo knots – that he got free on his own?"

"Yes he did. Poor old Derek, he was just about blowing a gasket by then. He tells me he informed Banfold that the horse had untied his own lead rope – and that all he got was an earful of abuse – 'I've known horses for forty years and I've never heard such rubbish, untying his own rope my eye' etc. etc."

"I can just imagine him saying all that," Sandra said ruefully, thinking of the rudeness we'd encountered.

"Derek had had enough. For the first time he bellowed back and he told the old man that if he wanted to take the horse back he would. I must say he sounded very guilty, telling me all this, he says he realises it seems childish now, but he just lashed out in retaliation for all the trouble Banfold had been causing."

"What did Banfold reply – did he say he'd report Derek to the police?" Jason was fascinated.

"How could he? Although he's the legal owner he gave Saracen as a present to his granddaughter. He could hardly report it as a theft, could he?"

"So – when Runaway was taken out of his field Banfold thought Derek Albany had done what he threatened," Sandra said. "And of course Trish and Derek didn't know the horse had been taken. And Helen was in France."

"So because all these stupid people are fighting and trying to outdo each other that poor, unwanted, beautiful horse was carted off yet again to be off-loaded who knows where." I was furious. "They all need their heads banging together! People like that – "

"Hold on Kate." Sandra looked at me. "It's a very sad story and all those people have been deeply hurt I would say."

I muttered and growled and Natalie patted my head and said "There, there, Tiger. Your precious baby didn't get hurt did he? The question is, having unravelled that lot Andrew, what's the next step?"

He turned to Sandra. "Would you like me to go and see the old man – "

"No," she said emphatically. "A carefully worded letter is what's called for now. What did Derek Albany want you to do?"

"He left it to me. They certainly don't want the horse. He was very offended that Banfold should think he was trying to sell it and says he wants no part of it at all. I think, as you say, a letter to the old man spelling it all out as clearly as possible, without entering into the family argument of course."

"And what about Runaway?" I burst out. "And me?"

"We'll tell him all about you and your dad's offer to buy the horse," Andrew said a little helplessly. "Though he doesn't sound the most approachable seller does he?"

"He'll tear that letter up and stamp on it," I said gloomily. "Then he'll send yet another lorry down here and he'll sell Runaway to just anyone with enough cash."

"I don't see what else we can do, Kate." Sandra looked at me anxiously. "He won't even let us in the door to talk face to face."

We'd finished the sandwiches and there didn't seem anything else to say. Andrew wanted to take Sandra over to his house and Nat was spending the afternoon with some friends at the swimming pool. I was all ready to waste mine just moping but Jason had other ideas.

"Come on then." He was busily counting his money. "The train goes in ten minutes."

"The – we're still going to see Mr Banfold?" I stared at him.

"Of course we are." He took off on his bike and I tore after him, excitement and terror pounding within me in equal quantities.

CHAPTER FOURTEEN

We were lucky with the train – we got to the station with minutes to spare and found it was a "slow" one stopping at a town just a few miles from Swallow Ridge. We took Sandra's map with us and, after unloading the bikes the other end, we sat studying it.

"It's pretty straightforward from here," Jason said, "although as you say Kate, the country lanes leading to the house twist and turn a fair bit. Are you ready?"

"Yup!" I tried to sound more chirpy than I was feeling. "I suppose Mr Banfold can only say no – oh look at that."

Jason tried to follow my gaze. "Where are you looking? The supermarket car park?"

"Mm. See the woman just locking the red car door? She's the housekeeper."

"From Swallow Ridge? Maybe that's a good thing. The old man might be more inclined to talk if she isn't there."

"I doubt it." My cheerfulness was fading fast. "It's more likely we won't even get the door opened. If Mr Banfold looks out and recognizes me he'll refuse to answer the bell."

"That's not the attitude." Jason sounded severe. "We're going to sort this mess out, he'll just have to listen. Be positive."

I was positive the afternoon was going to be another complete disaster but I kept quiet, smiled bravely, and got a fabulous grin in return.

"That's my girl. Let's get going, the housekeeper will be at least an hour won't she?"

I followed him out of the town and we were soon whizzing along familiar looking leafy lanes.

"It's just down here." I tried to call but my throat was so dry now we were this near, my voice came out in a croak.

Jason turned his head to look at me. "Are you all right?"

"Fine," I lied, feeling even more jelly legged and fuzzy brained than when I'd entered the ring at the Diamond show. "Just a bit nervous that's all."

"No need. You've got me this time." He winked broadly and I immediately felt better.

We pedalled our way slowly along Swallow Ridge's creamy gravel drive. I'd have liked to stop and explore the stable yard with its slate roof and quaint clock tower, but didn't dare in case Mr Banfold was watching. We leant the bikes neatly against a courtyard wall and walked to the heavy studded front door. My hands were clammy and I could almost feel my face going white, but Jason looked cool and confident. He stepped forward and rang the bell firmly. We waited a few moments. Birds sang in the trees all around the house and my heart thumped like a pneumatic drill. The door stayed shut. Jason tried again. We waited longer this time, then he tried a third time.

"Maybe the bell doesn't work," he suggested, looking at me hopefully.

"It did this morning," I pointed out. "The housekeeper answered it. I told you so, Mr Banfold's looked out, seen me, and refused to answer it."

"I don't think so. I haven't seen anyone at a window." He looked up. "Though there are an awful lot of windows I will say."

"Exactly. He's probaby sat at one of them looking at us, having made up his mind to waste no more of his precious time on us. He really is an arrogant old – "

"Sssh," Jason glanced round. "Let's not put his back up any further then. He could be out of course. His housekeeper may have dropped him off somewhere before we saw her."

I took a couple of steps back and gazed boldly at each and every window. They winked and glittered in the sun but none seemed to be looking back at me. "You could be right. What are we going to do now?"

"Mooch around and wait for him to come home," Jason said cheerfully. "We might see which field he kept Runaway in while he was here. Our horsethief could have left a clue that will convince

Banfold we're telling the truth."

"Could we have a quick look round the yard then?" I asked eagerly. "It's not in use of course, but it's such a lovely old one."

"OK. Come on." He limped at his usual rapid pace towards the mellow brick wall surrounding the stableyard.

I followed, admiring the ancient cobblestone and running my fingers along the warm, rough surface of the building.

There were ten big hunter boxes grouped to face inward on the yard.

"Look, the stables still have the old horses' names on the doors." I was whispering, I don't know why.

Jason shot me an amused glance. "Think there might be ghosts? We won't wake them even if there are."

I peeped over one of the doors. The stable was swept clean and bare, the lovely smell of straw and hay and horses completely vanished.

"I don't believe in ghosts," I said, more loudly this time "But hasn't it got a sad feel to it? Unhappy and lonely, as if the yard is mourning for the life that used to be here."

I saw Jason raise his eyebrows in surprise at my flight of fancy and turned away before he could tease me about it. As I did I distinctly heard a low moan and a faint, metallic rattle.

I spun round. "Don't take the mickey! How did you DO that Jason?"

To my astonishment he'd gone quite white. "I didn't – I – it wasn't me."

"So who's fooling around?" I strode angrily round the yard, peering deeply into each stable.

Jason gulped and joined in.

"There's no one else here." He looked at me. "It couldn't have been a ghost we heard could it – "

The sound came again, slightly louder.

"It's from behind the wall." He limped swiftly to an archwayed entrance. "Through here, I – oh hell!"

I ran to him and stopped short in dismay. The cobbled path dipped away from the back wall, sloping towards wooded grounds and paddocks. There, tight against the old brick was a wheelchair, tipped on its side, its rubber clad wheels spinning lightly. Much worse was the sight of the man who lay, face down, beside it, his thick silver hair and frail-looking body instantly recognisable.

"Mr Banfold!" I ran forward and knelt beside him. He moaned again and fluttered his hand against the moving spokes, the ring on his finger making the grating rattle we'd heard before. "Jason, what do we do?"

"Better not move him." He was examining the old man swiftly and gently. "In case he's broken any bones."

174

"No." The voice was weaker but it still had that incisive edge. "There is nothing broken I can tell. I am – just unable to get up. Help me."

I looked at Jason. "Shall I go and fetch someone?"

"There is no one." The old voice was stronger now. "They are all out. You do it."

I felt a grudging admiration for him, face down and helpless, yet still as bossy and dictatorial as ever.

Jason shrugged and slid his strong hands beneath the old man's shoulders. "If you say so. Kate, when I say "lift" will you hold his legs? I'll be taking his weight this end, it won't be too heavy. No wait, I'll have to put the chair to rights first."

He pulled the wheelchair gently away so it wasn't touching the old man, then raised it back on its wheels, running his hands over the framework to check it out. "Seems to be OK. Right, Mr Banfold, let's get you back aboard."

I held the man's bony legs as instructed and before I knew it Jason had lifted him cleanly off the cobblestones and settled him back into the chair as effortlessly as if he'd been a baby. Mr Banfold stretched his arms, grunting a little as he flexed his fingers.

"What's the matter?" I asked anxiously "That hurt you didn't it?"

"Just a little. Don't fuss." Colour was coming back into his face but there was no sign of an improvement in his manners.

Jason looked at him sternly. "She's not fussing. You could have been seriously hurt. We'll take you back to the house and phone your doctor. He'll want to check you over."

"I don't need checking over." The old man's voice was as irritable as ever but he looked pale and shaky, and when Jason turned the chair and started pushing it towards the house, he didn't argue any further.

"Is he all right Kate?" Jason couldn't see his face from behind the chair obviously.

"His eyes are shut and he's still not a very good colour." I was walking alongside.

"The poor old man's probably suffering from shock – a fall like that – he should never have been left alone."

"HE's not deaf you know." Mr Banfold's eyes snapped open. "I may be old and my legs don't work but that doesn't mean I can't hear you, young man. You have no idea how insulting it is to be treated like an idiot just because you're in a wheelchair."

I glanced quickly at Jason. He flushed angrily but pressed his lips together, refusing with great self-control not to upset the man any further by putting him right.

I tried to do the same. "We're certainly not treating you like that," I said, keeping my voice light. "We're simply concerned, that's all."

"No need to be. I was on my own because I chose to be. I sent them all out this afternoon, housekeeper, gardener, the lot. I wanted time on my own to think and I was just trying to get to my favourite spot when this – this happened."

It was the stableyard he'd been heading for. Compassion flooded through me as I realised this sad old man's happiest memories probably centred round the horses from Swallow Ridge's past. His son had been a keen horseman hadn't he, and the little girl Helen had ridden a pony when she visited Granddad. Our call at the house this morning had upset him as much as it had us and he'd tried to reach the old yard to calm himself and think things through. We'd reached the house and Jason manoevered the chair into the big square hall. It was oak panelled, hung with lovely old paintings and very, very grand.

"I'll need a phone please." Jason was still very polite. "And your doctor's number."

"In the study." Mr Banfold waved towards a door. "There's an address book on the desk. His number's in the front."

Jason moved quickly across the black and white chequered floor to the far side of the hall.

"Why is he limping?" the obnoxious old man

demanded. "Don't worry, I'll pay him for helping me, he doesn't have to pretend he's hurt himself doing it. One cripple here is enough."

That did it. I'd been making allowances for the man's age, the sad and tragic happenings in his past and the fact he'd just taken a tumble, but now he had gone too far.

"Mr Banfold!" I swung the chair sharply, forcing him to face me. "How DARE you say that. Is it just a habit of yours to think the worst of everyone?"

He opened his mouth to speak but I was in full spate and swept on regardless. I told him everything. I started with Jason's fight to get out of a wheelchair and walk, went on to Derek Albany's complete innocence in the theft of Runaway and ended with my opinion of his diabolical treatment of his family.

"You're telling me I've got everything wrong." He looked at me and for the first time his expression was of puzzlement not bitterness. "Derek's not a thief? And he didn't marry Trish for her money?"

"It certainly doesn't look like it. He didn't want the house you bought, and as I've told you he certainly didn't steal Runaway – Saracen Prince – to make money."

"And Helen – Helen didn't refuse the horse because she hates me?" He looked very old when he said that and my heart went out to the miserable old fellow.

"No, she doesn't hate you. She hates riding. She's a musician, Mr Banfold, not a showjumper. She's very talented apparently, you should be proud of her."

"I am. Oh I am. I just wanted to keep her here, to keep her – "

"She'll always come back," I said gently. "And it'll be much better if you let her go with your blessing because she'll WANT to come back, not just because you bribed her with an expensive horse. You can't solve everything with money you know."

Jason had returned from the study. "The doctor's on his way," he told Mr Banfold. "Though if you can take Tiger Kate's shock treatment you must be feeling fit. I could hear her even with the door shut."

Banfold smiled faintly "She's quite a girl. I haven't thanked you, either of you, for rescuing me. I'm sorry I was so rude and ungrateful."

The words sounded creaky as if he hadn't used the expression for a long time, but we could see he really meant it. We helped him into a chair in the drawing room, then there was a flurry of activity as the doctor, a nurse and the housekeeper all arrived simultaneously.

The nurse and doctor went straight to the old man, and the housekeeper, flapping slightly, started making tea, twittering about her employer sending her out and how she'd seen the doctor's car leaving town and she'd rushed home just in case. She obviously thought it odd that Jason and I should be inside the house and made it plain Mr Banfold wouldn't want us around any longer, so we drifted outside and got on our bikes.

We pedalled off thoughtfully and caught the next train home. I felt drained and a bit shaky, the result of all that shouting I dare say, and Jason did his best to cheer me.

"You did fantastically well." He lifted my chin and made an encouraging though hideous face at me. "You actually made that terrible old man LISTEN. I bet no one's achieved that for years."

"Not since his son died I expect," I agreed dolefully. "I can't say I feel great about it. All I've done is make him sad and me sadder."

"Why?" His dark eyes were full of concern. "He needed shouting at. Why does it make you unhappy?"

I fought to hold back the tears. "Because the reason we came here, the reason I tried so hard to see him is ruined now. I hope, I really hope, Mr Banfold and his family get back together, but as far as I'm concerned all it means is I've finally lost Runaway. Now his real owner knows where he is and how he got there, he'll be taken away from me and sold on. I've lost him, Jason."

CHAPTER FIFTEEN

H E STARED AT ME. "No you haven't. We didn't resolve it either way did we? What with finding the old man like that and getting him back to the house – "

"And I was so intent on putting him right about his judgment of people I didn't give myself time to sort out Runaway." I groaned and banged my forehead with clenched fists.

"Don't do that," Jason begged, pulling my hands away. "You were brilliant Kate. I heard you, telling him how wrong he was about folk, telling him how great Sandra and Andrew and everyone has been. Even using little old me as a shining example of One Who's Done Battle With A Wheelchair And Survived."

"Stop it." I was half laughing, half crying. "You make me sound awful. It was the things old Banfold said about you that set me off. I've never been so angry – "

"So angry you forgot to mention in your list what a terrific character YOU've been in all this." His voice was serious now and he was still holding my hands. "While you were telling him how badly he'd misjudged those around him you could have mentioned that."

"I just wish I'd mentioned my dad's offer to buy

Runaway," I moaned. "I might have caught him at a weak moment."

"Maybe. Still, give him time to think and perhaps he'll work it out for himself."

I tried to smile, but I didn't really believe it and my poor, long-suffering parents endured another evening of me weeping over the loss of Runaway. I cycled over to Falconhurst bright and early as usual the next morning though. Everyone there was in great high spirits.

"We've just seen the most wonderful sight in the world," Natalie explained.

I thought longingly of an official looking paper stating "Runaway Bay owned by Kate Harvey". "What is it?" I asked.

"A 'SOLD' sign." Nat paused for effect and when I didn't react, added impatiently, "Outside the Gray's house. Isn't it great?"

"Absolutely great," I agreed fervently. "So you'll all be able to stay at Falconhurst. You and your mum and the school and the horses?"

"For the present," Sandra came up, grinning. "It certainly takes any immediate pressure off, that's for sure, and who knows what the future will bring, eh Kate?"

I knew she meant Andrew, and I was glad for her. "Is there any news from Mr Banfold?" I asked. "He'll have got his letter this morning won't he?" I didn't mention our afternoon's adventure.

"It'll be an hour or so before he gets the post," Sandra said. "Don't hold your breath waiting for him to reply, Kate. That man is such a misery, it won't occur to him you're fretting."

I knew she was right and couldn't believe my outburst the day before would have done much to change things. I got on rather drearily with the chores and tried to put the whole episode out of my mind.

As usual, though, I couldn't stop thinking about Runaway and as soon as I could I sneaked off for a cuddle and a chat with him. My arms were round his neck and my face buried in his mane so I didn't hear Sandra at first when she called me.

"KATE!" She was running towards me across the field. "It's him. It's Mr Banfold."

"He's here?" My heart stopped, I'm sure it did. "He's come to take Runaway?"

"No. He's on the phone, he wants to speak to you. Kate, he says you went to see him, that you and Jason helped him. You funny creature, you didn't say a thing to us."

I ran back beside her. "I didn't want to tell you I had a major flare-up at him. You're always on about my temper."

"You only unleash it when it's deserved," she said, panting a little with the running. "And if Banfold wants a fight I shall tell him so."

That was brave of her, considering how she

hates a row herself.

Mr Banfold was still hanging on and sounding remarkably patient.

"Hullo Kate," he said.

"Good morning Mr Banfold," I replied politely, crossing my fingers and toes he didn't want Runaway back today. "How are you feeling?"

"My arm's a little sore but otherwise fine. I'm – I'm feeling grateful too."

"Oh?" I was startled, it wasn't what I expected.

"You and Jason did more than pick me up and dust me down. You cleaned a few scales from my eyes too."

"Scales?" I was sounding like Alexander the parrot but I didn't know what he meant by that.

"I can see a lot more clearly now. You made me look at things from a different angle. I phoned my family and – but you don't want to hear all that. What I wanted to get clear straight away is the horse."

"Runaway," I said faintly.

"Er – yes. Saracen Prince as was. I got your friend's letter this morning. It confirmed everything you told me and it also mentioned your father's offer to buy the horse for you. We'll sort out all the legal papers and so on but I wanted to tell you immediately – I accept the offer. Saracen – Runaway – is yours. Officially and legally yours."

I stared stupidly at the phone. My mouth

moved soundlessly. For some reason my voice wouldn't work.

"Kate?" Mr Banfold's old voice was anxious. "Are you there? I do realise of course that you could have just kept the horse and left me thinking the worst of my family. You acted honourably and I wish to do the same. Is that all right?"

I nodded and managed to croak "Yes. Oh yes. Thank you."

I heard him give a satisfied sigh. "I spoke to Helen after you'd gone. She's coming to see me. It's I who must thank you, Kate."

He said some more things about papers and a bill of sale and I nodded dumbly and uttered the odd squeak. When I put the phone back, Jason, Sandra and Natalie were all staring expectantly. I waved my arms wordlessly.

"Is everything all right. Kate, you didn't go this white when we thought we'd heard a ghost." Jason moved quickly to me. "What is it? What did he say?"

"He says – he says I can buy Runaway," I croaked.

They all cheered and Jason picked me up and whirled me round till I was dizzy.

"What's going on?" Andrew's kind, smiley face was at the door. "Is this because the Grays are moving back to a nice quiet estate where there are no nasty horses to upset them? You'll like your new neighbours, they're friends of mine, and they'll love living here. As soon as I told them about the locality they went straight round and talked the old miseries into selling.

"Your friends – oh Andrew!" Sandra stopped hugging me and ran to hug him. "I should have known you'd be behind it. You are wonderful. This is a double celebration actually."

"You'll never guess what else," Natalie beamed at him.

"Um," he pretended to think. "You've heard from Mr Banfold?"

"Andrew!" Sandra shrieked, "How do you know?"

"I got a call from Derek Albany early this morning. He wanted to know what brand of witchcraft we'd used on the old man. Says he got a phone call that was friendlier and more reasonable than he'd ever known. Derek actually received an apology for past treatment and Trish was over the moon at the way the old boy spoke to them both. She gave him the number of the friends Helen's staying with so he was able to make amends to his granddaughter too. And all that because of a visit Mr Banfold received from a certain young couple. I hope he was suitably civil to you as well."

"He was pretty nice," I grinned, pretending to be casual. "He's letting me buy Runaway, Andrew! Even though my dad's offer is way below what the horse is worth."

"For once in his life he's realised money's not the be-all and end-all." Andrew patted me on the back. "I told Derek and Trish it wasn't a witch but a tiger who'd got the old fellow to put his priorities in order."

"Hmm," Nat said darkly. "Seeing how much good Kate's done him I think he could have given her Runaway as a present."

"Oh no," I was shocked. "That way it wouldn't feel as though he was mine. This way – oh Nat, it's going to be GREAT!!"

And great it was. We spent the rest of the summer riding and schooling and entering shows. Jason continued with his lessons, his confidence in himself growing as he improved. He'd grown used to the Falconhurst teasing too, and was always happy to join in the banter.

Even Natalie, still not his greatest fan, commented on the change in him since he'd been with us.

"Before you learnt to ride you were such a moody thing," she told him, in that unsubtle way of hers, "and so touchy, we had to watch every word we said. But now I can almost tell what Kate sees in you."

"Thanks a lot." Jason flicked some water at her. "You're not as bad as you were back then either. It's done you and your crazy horse good to have some class competition from Kate and Runaway. You're not quite as cocky as you were."

"Oh yes I am," Nat retorted, then sighed as she realised what she'd said. "What I mean is – "

"A bit less meaning and a lot more working, you lot." Monkey's nice wrinkly face pretended to be severe. "Only two more days to the biggest Diamond Show of the season. That tack has got to look every bit as good as theirs or I'll want to know why."

In fact we looked better than anyone else, or at least I thought so. Even the usual butterfly stomach and jelly legs couldn't stop the feeling of joy and pride as I entered the ring and heard the announcement – 'Runaway Bay, owned and ridden by Miss Kate Harvey'. It was another terrifying-looking course but my confidence in my wonderful bay horse meant I could really go for it. Runaway went through the start and approached the first fence like a sleek dark rocket. I touched his sides and he rose, curving and stretching to land perfectly. Next was a flimsy-looking gate, easy enough, but several earlier competitors had knocked it down with the slightest of touches. I checked our pace and we cleared it with a comfortably safe margin, turning as we landed to put us in line with the formidable treble. Runaway was thoroughly enjoying himself as usual and we bounced through the combination, hearing the crowd gasp at the speed we were travelling. A hefty wall, a steepish bank and a coldly glittering water jump were no problem and we cantered through the finish with the sound of applause ringing in our ears. It was so like the daydream I'd indulged in the very first night I saw Runaway that I had to pinch myself to make sure it was real this time. I slid off my horse and was immediately surrounded by my friends. They were making such a joyous noise of congratulation that I barely heard a quiet voice say, "That was wonderful. I could never have done that."

I looked across to where a small, slim girl stood watching us. I knew I'd never seen her before but she looked strangely familiar and for a moment I wondered if I was back in my dream. Then I saw the wheelchair behind her.

"Helen?" I said.

"Hello Kate." She smiled warmly and the sombre likeness to her grandfather lessened. "Another win. Well done."

"I hope you don't mind me owning Runa – Saracen," I blurted anxiously. If I was her, I'd simply hate me, if you see what I mean.

"Oh no, I'm thrilled he's got the owner he deserves." She smiled again and put her hand on the shoulder of the old man in the wheelchair. "I've got my granddad back, that's what I wanted."

Mr Banfold's crusty old face softened instantly and I felt a lump in my throat when I saw the way he looked at her.

"Wh – what are you doing here?" I asked, the feeling of nervousness the old man induced still present.

"Cheering you on of course." Jason gave me his gorgeous grin, obviously unaffected by any such worry. "And discussing a little business with Sandra. Oh yes, and me."

"You?" I flung Runaway's rug over his loins. "What sort of business is this then?"

"You impressed me quite a lot that day at Swallow Ridge," Mr Banfold answered me. "Apart from knocking a bit of sense about my family into this stubborn old head, it also made me remember I'm not the only person in the world who's disabled. I'm old now of course, but there are thousands younger than me and what you told me about Jason and how he wanted to ride made me think about others like him, and indeed much worse off than him."

"Mr Banfold's been in touch with the RDA," Natalie chimed in eagerly. "And he's going to help us set up at Falconhurst."

"I'm going to train as an instructor", Jason said proudly. "That's in the long-term plan. Starting right away there'll be a manege, special facilities, expert tuition. Mr Banfold's put all sort of ideas to

Sandra."

"Where's the money coming from?" I asked bluntly. I thought it was a brilliant plan but you have to be practical.

"That's where I come in." The old man patted my hand and laughed. "You told me, quite rightly, that money can't solve everything, but it can help a little in this case."

"It sounds great." I was flabbergasted at the change in him. "What does your mum say, Nat?"

"She's over the moon. She's always wanted to get involved with lessons for the disabled but our teaching facilities have been so poor. With all this, and our nice new neighbours, Falconhurst is wonderful."

I'd always thought so and with the prospect of a certain future there for Runaway, me AND Jason, it was more than that it was sheer heaven. Mr Banfold invited us all to join him for a celebration drink. He and Helen went off with Sandra and Andrew to organise a bit of a party. Natalie and Rio, who were absolutely covered in rosettes, had to go back to the trailer first and Jason and I went too with Runaway. Jason helped me untack the bay horse and gave HIM a quick pat and ME a long hug.

"Stop it you two!" Natalie had seen us. "There's a newspaper reporter here to write about our success. Come and tell him all about yourselves."

We brushed ourselves down hurriedly and went to meet the journalist.

As we got near we heard my friend say, in her usual offbeat way, "Where are we from? Well, let me see, Kate and I are from Falconhurst, that's my mother's brilliant riding school. Rio is from Hampshire originally, and Runaway – you'll have to ask Kate." We could see her wicked grin. "She'll tell you all about Runaway – the Horse from Nowhere!"